Beran's heart took a queer jump. "Why must I go?"

Palafox inspected Beran with dispassionate appraisal. "Because now you are Panarch. If you had remained on Pao, Bustamonte would have killed you."

Looking across the chasm, Beran remembered the verdant landscape and blue seas of his homeworld with a pang. "When will I go back to Pao?" he asked in sudden anxiety.

Palafox looked swiftly down at him. "Do you want to be Panarch of Pao?"

"Yes," said Beran decidedly.

Palafox smiled. "Perhaps you may be granted your wish. But you must never forget that he who gets must give."

Also by Jack Vance
published by Tor Books

Araminta Station
Green Magic

JACK VANCE
THE LANGUAGES OF PAO

A TOM DOHERTY ASSOCIATES BOOK
NEW YORK

THE LANGUAGES OF PAO

Copyright © 1958 by Jack Vance; copyright © 1957 by Renown
Publications, Inc.

A TOR Book
Published by Tom Doherty Associates, Inc.
49 West 24 Street
New York, N.Y. 10010

Cover art by Maelo Cintron

ISBN: 0-812-55696-8   Can. ISBN: 0-812-55697-6

First Tor edition: May 1989

Printed in the United States of America

0 9 8 7 6 5 4 3 2 1

I

IN THE HEART OF the Polymark Cluster, circling the yellow star Auriol, is the planet Pao, with the following characteristics:

Mass:	1.73	(in standard units)
Diameter:	1.39	
Surface Gravity:	1.04	

The plane of Pao's diurnal rotation is the same as its plane of orbit; hence there are no seasons and the climate is uniformly mild. Eight continents range the equator at approximately equal intervals: Aimand, Shraimand, Vidamand, Minamand, Nonamand, Dronamand, Hivand and Impland, after the eight digits of the Paonese numerative system. Aimand, largest of the continents, has four times the area of Nonamand, the least. Only Nonamand, in the high southern latitudes, suffers an unpleasant climate.

An accurate census of Pao has never been made, but the great mass of the population—estimated at fifteen billion persons—lives in country villages.

The Paonese are a homogeneous people, of medium stature, fair-skinned with hair-color ranging from tawny-brown to brown-black, with no great variations of feature or physique. Paonese history previous to the reign of Panarch Aiello Panasper is uneventful. The first settlers, finding the planet hospitable, multiplied to an unprecedented density of population. Their system of life minimized social friction; there were no large wars, no plagues, no disasters except recurrent famine, which was endured with fortitude. A simple uncomplicated people were the Paonese, without religion or cult. They demanded small material rewards from life, but gave a correspondingly large importance to shifts of caste and status. They knew no competitive sports, but enjoyed gathering in enormous clots of ten or twenty million persons to chant the ancient drones. The typical Paonese farmed a small acreage, augmenting his income with a home craft or special trade. He showed small interest in politics; his hereditary ruler, the Panarch, exercised an absolute personal rule which reached out, through a vast civil service, into the most remote village. The word "career" in Paonese was synonymous to employment with the civil service. And, in general, the governmental was sufficiently efficient.

The language of Pao was derived from Waydalic, but molded into peculiar forms. The Paonese sentence did not so much describe an act as it presented a picture of a situation. There were no verbs, no adjectives; no formal word comparison such as *good, better, best*. The typical Paonese saw himself as a cork on a sea of a million waves, lofted, lowered, thrust aside by incomprehensible forces—if he thought of himself as a discrete personality at all. He held his ruler in awe, gave unquestioning obedience, and asked in return only dynastic continuity, for on Pao nothing must vary, nothing must change.

But the Panarch, absolute tyrant though he might be, was also forced to conform. Here lay the paradox: the single inner-directed individual of Pao was allowed vices unthinkable and abhorrent to the average man. But he might not appear gay or frivolous; he must hold himself aloof from friendship; he must show himself seldom in public places. Most important of all, he must never seem indecisive or uncertain. To do so would break the archetype.

II

PERGOLAI, AN ISLET in the Jhelianse Sea between Minamand and Dronamand had been pre-empted and coverted into an Arcadian retreat by Panarch Aiello Panasper. At the head of a meadow bordered by Paonese bamboo and tall myrrh trees stood Aiello's lodge, an airy structure of white glass, carved stone and polished wood. The plan was simple: a residential tower, a service wing, and an octagonal pavilion with a pink marble dome. Here in the pavilion, at a carved ivory table, sat Aiello to his midday repast, wearing the Utter Black of his position. He was a large man, small-boned, well-fleshed. His silver-gray hair shone fine as a baby's; he had a baby's clear skin and wide unwinking stare. His mouth drooped, his eyebrows arched high, conveying a perpetual sense of sardonic and skeptical inquiry.

To the right sat his brother Bustamonte,

bearing the title Ayudor—a smaller man, with a shock of coarse dark hair, quick black eyes, knobs of muscles in his cheeks. Bustamonte was energetic beyond the usual Paonese norm. He had toured two or three nearby worlds, returning with a number of alien enthusiasms which had gained him the dislike and distrust of the Paonese population.

On Aiello's other side sat his son, Beran Panasper, the Medallion. He was a thin child, hesitant and diffident, with fragile features and long black hair, resembling Aiello only in his clear skin and wide eyes.

Across the table sat a score of other men: functionaries of the government, petitioners, three commercial representatives from Mercantil, and a hawk-faced man in brown and gray who spoke to no one.

Aiello was attended by special maids wearing long gowns striped with black and gold. Each dish served him was first tasted by Bustamonte—a custom residual from times when assassination was the rule rather than the exception. Another manifestation of this ancient caution could be found in the three Mamarone standing vigilant behind Aiello. These were enormous creatures tattoed dead-black—neutraloids. They wore magnificent turbans of cerise and green, tight pantaloons of the same colors, chest emblems of white silk and silver, and carried shields of refrax to be locked in front of the Panarch in the event of danger.

Aiello morosely nibbled his way through the meal and finally indicated that he was ready to conduct the business of the day.

Vilnis Therobon, wearing the ocher and purple of Public Welfare, arose and came to stand before the Panarch. He stated his problem: the cereal farmers of South Impland savannahs were beset by drought; he, Therobon, wished to bring water from across the Central Impland watershed, but had been unable to work out a satisfactory arrangement with the Minster of Irrigation. Aiello listened, asked a question or two, then, in a brief sentence, authorized a water-purification plant at the Koroi-Sherifte Isthmus, with a ten-thousand mile pipe-line network to take the water where needed.

The Minister of Public Health spoke next. The population of Dronomand's central plain had expanded past available housing. To build new dwellings would encroach upon land assigned to food production, and would hasten the famine already threatening. Aiello, munching a crescent of pickled melon, advised transportation of a million persons weekly to Nonamand, the bleak southern continent. In addition, all infants arriving to parents with more than two children should be subaqueated. These were the classical methods of population control; they would be accepted without resentment.

Young Beran watched with fascination, awed
by the vastness of his father's power. He was
seldom allowed to witness state business, for
Aiello disiked children and showed only small
concern for the upbringing of his son. Recently the Ayudor Bustamonte had interested
himself in Beran, talking for hours on end,
until Beran's head grew heavy and his eyes
drooped. They played odd games which bewildered Beran and left with him a peculiar
uneasiness. And of late there had been blank
spaces in his mind, lapses of memory.

As Beran sat now at the ivory table in the
pavilion, he held a small unfamiliar object in
his hand. He could not recall where he had
found it, but it seemed as if there were something he must do. He looked at his father, and
felt a sudden hot panic. Bustamonte was looking at him, frowning. Beran felt awkward and
pulled himself erect in his chair. He must
watch and listen, as Bustamonte had instructed
him. Furtively, he inspected the object he held
in his hand. It was at once familiar and strange.
As if in recollection from a dream, he knew he
had use for his object—and again came the
wave of panic.

He tasted a bit of toasted fish-tail, but as
usual lacked appetite. He felt the brush of
eyes; someone was watching him. Turning his
head, he met the gaze of the stranger in brown
and gray. The man had an arresting face, long

and thin with a high forehead, a wisp of mustache, a nose like the prow of a ship. His hair was glossy black, thick and short as fur. His eyes were set deep; his gaze, dark and magnetic, awoke all of Beran's uneasiness. The object in his hand felt heavy and hot. He wanted to fling it down, but could not.

The last man to be heard was Sigil Paniche, business representative from Mercantil, the planet of a nearby sun. Paniche was a thin man, quick and clever, with copper-colored skin and burnished hair, which he wore wound into knobs and fastened with turquoise clasps. He was a typical Mercantil, a salesman and a trader, as essentially urban as the Paonese were people of soil and sea. His world sold to the entire cluster; Mercantil space-barges roved everywhere, delivering machinery, vehicles, aircraft, communication equipment, tools, weapons, power-generators, returning to Mercantil with foodstuffs, luxury hand-crafts and whatever raw material might be cheaper to import than to synthesize.

Bustamonte whispered to Aiello, who shook his head. Bustamonte whispered more urgently; Aiello turned him a slow caustic side-glance. Bustamonte sat back sullenly.

At a signal from Aiello, the captain of the Mamarone guard addressed the table in his soft scraped-steel voice. "By the Panarch's order, all those who have completed their business will depart."

Across the table, only Sigil Paniche, his two aides, and the stranger in brown and gray remained.

The Mercantil moved to a chair opposite Aiello; he bowed, seated himself, his aides coming to stand at his back.

Panarch Aiello spoke an off-hand greeting; the Mercantil responded in broken Paonese.

Aiello toyed with a bowl of brandied fruit, appraising the Mercantil. "Pao and Mercantil have traded for many centuries, Sigil Paniche."

The Mercantil bowed. "We fulfill the exact letter of our contracts—this is our creed."

Aiello laughed shortly. "Trade with Pao has enriched you."

"We trade with twenty-eight worlds, Supremacy."

Aiello leaned back in his chair. "There are two matters I wish to discuss with you. You have just heard our need for water on Impland. We require an installation to demineralize an appropriate quantity of ocean-water. You may refer this matter to your engineers."

"I am at your orders, sir."*

---

*The Paonese and Mercantil languages were as disparate as the two ways of living. The Panarch, making the statement, "There are two matters I wish to discuss with you," used words which, accurately rendered, would read: *"Statement-of-importance (a single word in Paonese)—in a state of readiness—two; ear—of*

Aiello spoke in a level emotionless voice, almost casual. "We have ordered from you, and you have delivered, large quantities of military equipment."

Sigil Paniche bowed agreement. With no outward sign or change, he suddenly seemed uneasy. "We fuliflled the exact requirements of your order."

"I cannot agree with you," Aiello responded.

Sigil Paniche became stiff; his words were even more formal than before, "I assure Your Supremacy that I personally checked delivery. The equipment was exactly as described in order and invoice."

Aiello went on in his coldest tones. "You delivered sixty-four* barrage monitors, 512 patrol flitters, a large number of multiple resonators, energetics, wasps and hand-weapons. These accord with the original order."

Mercantil—*in a state of readiness;* mouth—or this person here—*in a state of volition.*" The italicized words represent suffixes of condition.

The necessary paraphrasing makes the way of speaking seem cumbersome. But the Paonese sentence, *"Rhomel-en-shrai bogal-Mercantil-nli-en mous-es-nli-ro,"* requires only three more phonemes than, "There are two matters I wish to discuss with you."

The Mercantil express themselves in neat quanta of precise information. "I am at your orders, sir." Literally translated this is: *"I—Ambassador—here-now gladly-obey the just spoken-orders of-you—Supreme Royalty—here-now heard and understood."*

*The Paonese number system is based on the number 8. Hence, a Panonese 100 is 64, 1000 is 512, etc.

"Exactly, sir."

"However, you knew the purpose behind this order."

Sigil Paniche bowed his copper-bright head. "You refer to conditions on the planet Batmarsh."

"Just so. The Dolberg dynasty has been eliminated. A new dynasty, the Brumbos, have assumed power. New Batch rulers customarily undertake military ventures."

"Such is the tradition," agreed the Mercantil.

"You have supplied these adventurers with armament."

Sigil Paniche once again agreed. "We sell to any who will buy. We have done so for many years—you must not reproach us for this."

Aiello raised his eyebrows. "I do not do so. I reproach you for selling us standard models while offering the Brumbo Clan equipment against which you guarantee we will be powerless."

Sigil Paniche blinked. "What is the source of your information?"

"Must I divest myself of every secret?"

"No, no," exclaimed Paniche. "Your allegations, however, seem mistaken. Our policy is absolute neutrality."

"Unless you can profit by double-dealing."

Sigil Paniche drew himself erect. "Supremacy, I am official representative of Mercantil on Pao. Your statements to me, therefore, must be regarded as formal insults."

Aiello appeared to be faintly surprised. "Insult a Mercantil? Preposterous!"

Sigil Paniche's skin burnt vermilion.

Bustamonte whispered in Aiello's ear. Aiello shrugged, turned back to the Mercantil. His voice was cool, his words carefully measured. "For the reasons I have stated, I declare that the Mercantil contract has not been fulfilled. The merchandise will not perform its function. We will not pay."

Sigil Paniche affirmed, "The delivered articles meet the contractural specifications!" By his lights nothing more need be said.

"But they are useless to our need, a fact known on Mercantil."

Sigil Paniche's eyes gleamed. "No doubt Your Supremacy has considered the long-range effects of such a decision."

Bustamonte could not restrain a retort. "Better had the Mercantil consider the long-range effect of double-dealing."

Aiello made a small gesture of annoyance, and Bustamonte sat back.

Sigil Paniche looked over his shoulder to his two subordinates: they exchanged emphatic whispers. Then Paniche asked, "May I inquire as to what 'long-range effects' the Ayudor alluded?"

Aiello nodded. "I direct your attention to the gentleman at your left hand."

All eyes swung to the stranger in brown and

gray. "Who is this man?" Sigil Paniche asked sharply. "I do not recognize his clothes."

Aiello was served a bowl of green syrup by one of the black and gold-clad maidens. Bustamonte dutifully sampled a spoonful. Aiello drew the bowl close to him, sipped. "This is Lord Palafox. He is here to offer us advice." He sipped once more from the bowl, pushed it aside. The maiden quickly removed it.

Sigil Paniche surveyed the stranger with cold hostility. His aides muttered to each other. Bustamonte sat slumped into his seat.

"After all," said Aiello, "if we can not rely upon Mercantil for protection, we must seek elsewhere."

Sigil Paniche once more turned to whisper with his counselors. There was a hushed argument; Paniche snapped his fingers in emphasis, the counselors bowed and became silent. Paniche turned back to Aiello. "Your Supremacy naturally will act as he thinks best. I must point out that the products of Mercantil are surpassed nowhere."

Aiello glanced at the man in brown and gray. "I am not disposed to dispute this point. Lord Palafox might have something to say."

Palafox, however, shook his head.

Paniche motioned to one of his subordinates, who advanced reluctantly. "Allow me to display one of our new developments." The counselor handed him a case, from which Paniche withdrew a pair of small transparent hemispheres.

The neutraloid bodyguards, at the sight of the case, had leapt in front of Aiello with their refrax shields; Sigil Paniche grimaced painfully. "No need for alarm—there is no danger here."

He displayed the hemispheres to Aiello, then placed them over his eyes. "Our new optidynes! They function either as microscope or telescope! The enormous range of their power is controlled by the ocular muscles and the eyelids. Truly marvelous! For instance"—he turned, looked out the window of the pavilion— "I see quartz crystals in the stones of the sea-wall. A gray chit stands under that far funella bush." He turned his gaze to his sleeve. "I see the threads, the fibers of the threads, the laminae of the fibers."

He looked at Bustamonte. "I note the pores of the Ayudor's estimable nose. I observe several hairs in his nostril." He glanced at the Medallion, carefully avoiding the solecism of staring at Aiello. "The brave lad is excited. I count his pulse: one, two, three, four, five, six, seven, eight, eleven, twelve, thirteen. . . . He holds a tiny object between his fingers, no larger than a pill." He turned, inspected the man in gray. "I see . . ." he stared; then with a sudden gesture, removed the optidynes from his eyes.

"What did you see?" Bustamonte inquired.

Sigil Paniche studied the tall man in perturbation and awe. "I saw his sign. The tattoo of a Breakness wizard!"

The words seemed to arouse Bustamonte. He glared in accusation at Aiello, gave Palafox a look of loathing, then glowered down at the carved ivory of the table.

"You are correct," said Aiello. "This is Lord Palafox, Dominie of Breakness Institute."

Sigil Paniche bowed his head frigidly. "Will Your Supremacy allow me a question?"

"Ask what you will."

"What does Lord Palafox do here on Pao?"

Aiello said blandly, "He came at my behest. I need expert advice. Certain of my confidants"—he glanced rather contemptuously toward Bustamonte—"feel that we can buy Mercantil cooperation. He believes that for a price you will betray the Brumbos of Batmarsh in the same way you have already betrayed us."

Sigil Paniche said in a brittle voice, "We deal in all types of merchandise. We can be engaged for special research."

Aiello twisted his pink mouth into a sneer of repugnance. "I would rather deal with Lord Palafox."

"Why are you telling me this?"

"I would not have your syndics think that their treachery goes unnoticed."

Sigil Paniche made a great effort. "I urge you to reconsider. In no way have we cheated you. We delivered exactly what was ordered. Mercantil has served you well in the past—we hope to serve you in the future. If you deal with Breakness, think what the bargain entails!"

"I have made no bargains with Lord Palafox," said Aiello, with a swift glance toward the man in brown and gray.

"Ah, but you will—and, if I may speak openly . . ." He waited.

"Speak," said Aiello.

". . . to your eventual dismay." He became emboldened. "Never forget, Supremacy, that they build no weapons on Breakness. They make no application of their science." He looked to Palafox. "Is this not true?"

"Not altogether," replied Palafox. "A Dominie of the Institute is never without his weapons."

"And Breakness manufactures weapons for export?" Paniche persisted.

"No," answered Palafox with a slight smile. "It is well-known that we manufacture only knowledge and men."

Sigil Paniche turned to Aiello. "Only weapons can guard you against the fury of the Brumbos. Why not examine, at least, some of our new products?"

"This can do no harm," Bustamonte urged.

"And perhaps we will not require Palafox after all."

Aiello turned him a peevish glance, but Sigil Paniche already was displaying a globe-shaped projector with a hand grip. "This is one of our most ingenious developments."

The Medallion Beran, watching in absorption, felt a sudden quiver, a pang of indescribable alarm. Why? How? What? He must leave the pavilion, he must go! But he could not move from his seat.

Paniche was directing his tool toward the pink marble dome. "Observe, if you will." The top half of the room went black, as if concealed by a black shutter, as if snatched from existence. "The device seeks out, attracts and absorbs energy of the visual phase," explained the Mercantil. "It is invaluable for the confusion of an adversary."

Beran turned his head, looked helplessly toward Bustamonte.

"Now notice!" cried Sigil Paniche. "I turn this knob here . . ." He turned the knob; the room was blotted out entirely.

Bustamonte's cough was the only sound to be heard.

Then there was a hiss of surprise, a rustle of movement, a choking sound.

Light returned to the pavilion. A great horrified gasp sounded; all eyes went to the Panarch. He lay back into his pink silk divan.

His leg jerked up, kicked, set dishes and flagons on the table rattling.

"Help, doctor!" cried Bustamonte. "To the Panarch!"

Aiello's fists beat a spasmodic tattoo on the tabletop; his eyes went dim, his head fell forward in the complete lassitude of death.

III

THE DOCTORS gingerly examined Aiello, a gross hulk with arms and legs sprawled in four directions. Beran, the new Panarch, Deified Breath of the Paonese, Tyrant-Absolute of Eight Continents, Ocean-Master, Suzerain of the System and Acknowledged Leader of the Universe (among his other honorary titles), sat fidgeting, evidencing neither comprehension nor grief. The Mercantil stood in a taut group, muttering to each other; Palafox, who had not moved from his seat at the table, watched without interest.

Bustamonte, now Ayudor-Senior, lost no time in asserting the authority which, as regent for the new Panarch, he might be expected to employ. He waved his hand; a squad of Mamarone leapt to stations surrounding the pavilion.

"None will leave," declared Bustamonte,

"until these tragic circumstances are clarified." He turned to the doctors. "Have you determined the cause of death?"

The first of the three doctors bowed. "The Panarch succumbed to poison. It was administered by a sting-missile, thrust into the left side of his throat. The poison. . . ." He consulted the dials, the shadow-graphs and color-wheels of an analyzer into which his colleagues had inserted samples of Aiello's body-fluids. "The poison appears to be a mepothanax derivative, extin most probably."

"In that case," said Bustamonte, and his gaze swung from the huddle of Mercantil traders to the grave Lord Palafox, "the crime was committed by someone in this room."

Sigil Paniche diffidently approached the corpse. "Allow me to examine this sting."

The chief doctor indicated a metal plate. Here rested the black sting with its small white bulb.

Sigil Paniche's face was strained. "This object is that which I glimpsed in the hand of the Medallion, no more than a few moments ago."

Bustamonte succumbed to rage. His jowls went pink, his eyes swam with fire. "This accusation from you—a Mercantil swindler! You accuse the lad of killing his father?"

Beran began to whimper; his head wobbled from side to side. "Quiet," hissed Bustamonte. "The nature of the deed is clear!"

"No, no," protested Sigil Paniche, and all the Mercantil stood blanched and helpless.

"There is no room for doubt," Bustamonte stated inexorably. "You came to Pergolai aware that your duplicity had been discovered. You were resolved to evade the penalties."

"This is nonsense!" cried the Mercantil. "How could we plan so idiotic an act?"

Bustamonte ignored the protest. In a voice of thunder he continued. "The Panarch would not be mollified. You hid yourself in darkness, you killed the great leader of the Paonese!"

"No, no!"

"But you will derive no benefit from the crime! I, Bustamonte, am even less placable than Aiello! As my first act I pronounce judgment upon you."

Bustamonte held up his arm, palm outward, fingers clenched over thumb—the traditional death-signal of the Paonese. He called to the commander of the Mamarone. "Subaqueate these creatures!" He glanced into the sky; the sun was low. "Make haste, before sundown!"

Hurriedly, for a Paonese superstition forbade killing during the hours of darkness, the Mamarone carried the traders to a cliff overlooking an arm of the sea. Their feet were thrust into ballasted tubes, they were flung out through the air. They struck the water, sank, and the surface was calm as before.

Twenty minutes later, by order of Bustamonte, the body of Aiello was brought forth. Without ceremony it was weighted and cast after the Mercantil. Once again the sea showed a quick white blossom of foam; once again it rolled quiet and blue.

The sun hovered at the rim of the sea. Bustamonte, Ayudor-Senior of Pao, walked with nervously energetic steps along the terrace.

Lord Palafox sat nearby. At each end of the terrace stood a Mamarone, fire-sting aimed steadily at Palafox, to thwart any possible act of violence.

Bustamonte stopped short in front of Palafox. "My decision was wise—I have no doubt of it!"

"What decision is this?"

"In connection with the Mercantil."

Palafox considered. "You may now find trade relations difficult."

"Pah! What do they care for the lives of three men so long as there is profit to be obtained?"

"Very little, doubtless."

"These men were cheats and swindlers. They deserved no more than they received."

"In addition," Palafox pointed out, "the crime has been followed by an appropriate penalty, with no lack of equilibrium to disturb the public."

"Justice has been done," said Bustamonte stiffly.

Palafox nodded. "The function of justice, after all, is to dissuade any who might wish to perform a like misdeed. The execution constitutes such a dissuasion."

Bustamonte swung on his heel, paced up and down the terrace. "It is true that I acted partly from consideration of expediency."

Palafox said nothing.

"In all candor," said Bustamonte, "I admit that the evidence points to another hand in the affair, and the major element of the difficulty remains, like the bulk of an iceberg."

"What difficulty is this?"

"How shall I deal with young Beran?"

Palafox stroked his lean chin. "The question must be considered in its proper perspective."

"I fail to understand you."

"We must ask ourselves, did Beran actually kill the Panarch?"

Protruding his lips, bulging his eyes, Bustamonte contrived to become a grotesque hybrid of ape and frog. "Undoubtedly!"

"Why should he do so?"

Bustamonte shrugged. "Aiello had no love for Beran. It is doubtful if the child were actually fathered by Aiello."

"Indeed?" mused Lord Palafox. "And who might be the father?"

Bustamonte shrugged once more. "The Divine Petraia was not altogether fastidious in her indiscretions, but we will never know the truth, since a year ago Aiello ordained her subaqueation. Beran was grief-stricken, and here might be the source of the crime."

"Surely you do not take me for a fool?" Palafox asked, smiling a peculiar fixed smile.

Bustamonte looked at him in startlement. "Eh? What's this?"

"The execution of this deed was precise. The child appeared to be acting under hypnotic compulsion. His hand was guided by another brain."

"You feel so?" Bustamonte frowned. "Who might such 'another' be?"

"Why not the Ayudor-Senior?"

Bustamonte halted in his pacing, then laughed shortly. "This is fantasy indeed! What of yourself?"

"I gain nothing from Aiello's death," said Palafox. "He asked me here to a specific purpose. Now he is dead, and your own policy faces a different direction. There is no further need for me."

Bustamonte held up his hand. "Not so fast. Today is not yesterday. The Mercantil, as you suggest, may prove hard to deal with. Perhaps you will serve me as you might have served Aiello."

Palafox rose to his feet. The sun was settling past the far horizon into the sea; it swam orange and distorted in the thick air. A breeze tinkled among glass bells and drew sad flute-sounds from an aeolian harp; feathery cycads sighed and rustled.

The sun flattened, halved, quartered.

"Watch now!" said Palafox. "Watch for the green flash!"

The last fiery bar of red sank below the horizon; then came a flickering shaft of pure green, changing to blue, and the sunlight was gone.

Bustamonte spoke in a heavy voice, "Beran must die. The fact of particide is clear."

"You over-react to the situation," observed Palafox mildly. "Your remedies are worse than the ailment."

"I act as I think necessary," snapped Bustamonte.

"I will relieve you of the child," said Palafox. "He may return with me to Breakness."

Bustamonte inspected Palafox with simulated surprise. "What will you do with young Beran? The idea is ridiculous. I am prepared to offer you a draft of females to augment your prestige, but now I give orders in regard to Beran."

Palafox looked away into the dusk, smiling. "You fear that Beran will become a weapon against you. You want no possible challenge."

"It would be banal to deny it."

Palafox stared into the sky. "You need not fear him. He would remember nothing."

"What is your interest in this child?" demanded Bustamonte.

"Consider it a whim."

Bustamonte was curt. "I must disoblige you."

"I make a better friend than enemy," Palafox said softly.

Bustamonte stopped short in his tracks. He nodded suddenly amiable. "Perhaps I will reconsider. After all, the child can hardly cause trouble. . . . Come along, I will take you to Beran; we will observe his reaction to the idea."

Bustamonte marched off, rocking on his short legs. Smiling faintly, Palafox followed.

At the portal, Bustamonte muttered briefly to the captain of the Mamarone. Palafox, coming after, paused beside the tall black neutraloid, let Bustamonte proceed out of earshot. He spoke, tilting his head to look up into the harsh face.

"Suppose I were to make you a true man once more—how would you pay me?"

The eyes glowed, muscles rippled under the black skin. The neutraloid replied in the strange soft voice. "How would I pay you? By smashing you, by crushing your skull. I am more than a man, more than four men—why should I want the return of weakness?"

"Ah," marveled Palafox. "You are not prone to weakness?"

"Yes," sighed the neutraloid, "indeed I have

a flaw." He showed his teeth in a ghastly grin. "I take an unnatural joy in killing; I prefer nothing to the strangling of small pale men."

Palafox turned away, entered the pavilion.

The door closed behind him. He looked over his shoulder. The captain stood glaring through the transparent panel. Palafox looked to the other entrances; Mamarone stood at vigilance everywhere.

Bustamonte sat in one of Aiello's black foam chairs. He had flung a black cloak over his shoulders, the Utter Black of a Panarch.

"I marvel at you men of Breakness," said Bustamonte. "Your daring is remarkable! So casually do you put yourselves into desperate danger!"

Palafox shook his head gravely. "We are not so rash as we seem. No Dominie walks aboard without means to protect himself."

"Do you refer to your reputed wizardry?"

Palafox shook his head. "We are not magicians. But we have surprising weapons at our command."

Bustamonte surveyed the brown and gray costume which afforded no scope for concealment. "Whatever your weapons, they are not now in evidence."

"I hope not."

Bustamonte drew the black cloak over his knees. "Let us put ambiguity aside."

"Gladly."

"I control Pao. Therefore I call myself Panarch. What do you say to that?"

"I say that you have performed an exercise in practical logic. If you now bring Beran to me, the two of us will depart and leave you to the responsibilities of your office."

Bustamonte shook his head. "Impossible."

"Impossible? Not at all."

"Impossible for my purpose. Pao is ruled by continuity and tradition. Public emotion demands Beran's accession. He must die, before the news of Aiello's death reaches the world."

Palafox thoughtfully fingered the black mark of his mustache. "In that case it is already too late."

Bustamonte froze. "What do you say?"

"Have you listened to the broadcast from Eiljanre? The announcer is speaking at this moment."

"How do you know?" demanded Bustamonte.

Palafox indicated the sound-control in the arm of Bustamonte's chair. "There is the means to prove me wrong."

Bustamonte thrust down the knob. A voice issued from the wall, thick with synthetic emotion. "Pao, grieve! All Pao, mourn! The great Aiello, our noble Panarch is gone! Dole, dole, dole! Bewildered we search the sad sky, and our hope, our only sustention in this tragic hour is Beran, the brave new Panarch! Only let his reign prove as static and glorious as that of great Aiello!"

Bustamonte swung upon Palafox like a small black bull. "How did the news get abroad?"

Palafox replied with easy carelessness. "I myself released it."

Bustamonte's eyes glittered. "When did you do this? You have been under constant surveillance."

"We Breakness dominie," said Palafox, "are not without subterfuge."

The voice from the wall droned on. "Acting under the orders of Panarch Beran, the Mamarone have efficiently subaqueated the responsible criminals. Ayudor Bustamonte is serving Beran with wholehearted loyalty, and will help maintain equilibrium."

Bustamonte's fury seethed to the surface. "Do you think you can thwart me by such a trick?" He signaled the Mamarone. "You wished to join Beran. So you shall—in life and, at tomorrow's first light, in death."

The guards were at Palafox's back. "Search this man!" cried Bustamonte. "Inspect him with care!"

The guards subjected Palafox to a most minute scrutiny. Every stitch of his clothes was examined; he was patted and prodded with complete lack of regard for dignity.

Nothing was discovered; no tool, weapon or instrument of any kind. Bustamonte watched the search in unashamed fascination, and seemed disappointed at the negative result.

"How is this?" he asked scornfully. "You, a Wizard of Breakness Institute! Where are the devices, the infallible implements, the mysterious energetics?"

Palafox, who had submitted to the search without emotion, replied in a pleasant voice, "Alas, Bustamonte, I am not at liberty to answer your questions."

Bustamonte laughed coarsely. He motioned to the guard. "Take him to confinement."

The neutraloids seized Palafox's arms.

"One final word," said Palafox, "for you will not see me again on Pao."

Bustamonte agreed. "Of this I am sure."

"I came at Aiello's wish to negotiate a contract."

"A dastardly mission!" Bustamonte exclaimed.

"Rather an exchange of surpluses to satisfy each of our needs," said Palafox. "My wisdom for your population."

"I have no time for abstruseness." Bustamonte motioned to the guards. They urged Palafox toward the door.

"Allow me to say," spoke Palafox gently. The guards paid him no heed. Palafox made a small twitch, the neutraloids cried out and sprang away from him.

"What's this?" cried Bustamonte, jumping to his feet.

"He burns! He radiates fire!"

Palafox spoke in his quiet voice, "As I say, we will not meet again on Pao. But you will need me, and Aiello's bargain will seem very reasonable. And then you must come to Breakness." He bowed to Bustamonte, turned to the guards. "Come, now we will go."

IV

BERAN SAT with his chin on the window sill,
looking out into the night. The surf phospho-
resced on the beach, the stars hung in great
frosty clots. Nothing else could be seen.

The room was high in the tower; it seemed
very dreary and bleak. The walls were bare
fiber; the window was heavy cleax; the door
fitted into the aperture without a seam. Beran
knew the room for what it was—a confinement
chamber.

A faint sound came from below, the husky
grunting of a neutraloid's laugh. Beran was
sure that they were laughing at him, at the
miserable finale to his existence. Tears rose
to his eyes, but, in the fashion of Paonese
children, he made no other show of emotion.

There was a sound at the door. The lock
whirred, the door slid back. In the opening

stood two neutraloids, and, between them, Lord Palafox.

Beran came hopefully forward—but the attitudes of the three halted him. The neutraloids shoved Palafox forward. The door whirred shut. Beran stood in the center of the room, crestfallen and dejected.

Palafox glanced around the room, seeming instantly to appraise every detail. He put his ear to the door, listened, then took three long elastic strides to the window. He looked out. Nothing to be seen, only stars and surf. He touched his tongue to a key area on the inside of his cheek; an infinitesimal voice, that of the Eiljanre announcer, spoke inside his inner ear. The voice was excited. "Word has reached us from Ayudor Bustamonte on Pergolai: serious events! In the treacherous attack upon Panarch Aiello, the Medallion was likewise injured, and his survival is not at all likely! The most expert doctors of Pao are in constant attendance. Ayudor Bustamonte asks that all join to project a wave of hope for the stricken Medallion!"

Palafox extinguished the sound with a second touch of his tongue; he turned to Beran, motioned. Beran came a step or two closer. Palafox bent to his ear, whispered, "We're in danger. Whatever we say is heard. Don't talk, just watch me—and move quickly when I give the signal!"

Beran nodded. Palafox made a second inspection of the room, rather more slowly than before. As he went about his survey, a section of the door became transparent; an eye peered through.

In sudden annoyance Palafox raised his hand, then restrained himself. After a moment the eye disappeared, the wall became once more opaque.

Palafox sprang to the window; he pointed his forefinger. A needle of incandescence darted forth, cut a hissing slot through the cleax. The window fell loose, and before Palafox could catch it, disappeared into the darkness.

Palafox whispered, "Over here now! Quick!" Beran hesitated. "Quick!" whispered Palafox. "Do you want to live? Up on my back, quick!"

From below came the thud of feet, voices growing louder.

A moment later the door slid back; three Mamarone stood in the doorway. They stopped, stared all around, then ran to the open window.

The captain turned. "Below, to the grounds! It's deep water for all, if they have escaped!"

When they searched the gardens they found no trace of Palafox or Beran. Standing in the starlight, darker than the darkness, they argued in their soft voices, and presently reached a decision. Their voices ceased; they themselves slid away through the night.

Any collocation of persons, no matter
how numerous, how scant, how even their
homogeneity, how firmly they profess common doctrine, will presently reveal themselves to consist of small groups espousing
variant versions of the common creed, and
these sub-groups will manifest sub-sub-
groups, and so to the final limit of the
single individual, and even in this single
person conflicting tendencies will express
themselves.

—Adam Ostwald: *Human Society*.

THE PAONESE, in spite of their fifteen billion,
comprised as undifferentiated a group as could
be found in the human universe. Nevertheless,
to the Paonese the traits in common were taken
for granted and only the distinctions, minuscule
though they were, attracted attention.

In this fashion the people of Minamand—and especially those in the capitol city of Eiljanre—were held to be urbane and frivolous. Hivand, flattest and most featureless of the continents, exemplified bucolic naïveté. The people of Nonamand, the bleak continent to the south, bore the reputation of dour thrift and fortitude; while the inhabitants of Vidamand, who grew grapes and fruits, and bottled almost all the wine of Pao, were considered largehearted and expansive.

For many years, Bustamonte had maintained a staff of secret informants, stationed through the eight continents. Early in the morning, walking the airy gallery of the Pergolai lodge, he was beset by worry. Events were not proceeding at their optimum. Only three of the eight continents seemed to be accepting him as *de facto* Panarch. These were Vidamand, Minamand and Dronomand. From Aimand, Shraimand, Nonaman, Hivand and Impland, his agents reported a growing tide of recalcitrance.

There was no suggestion of active rebellion, no parades or public meetings. Paonese dissatisfaction expressed itself in surliness, a work-slowdown throughout the public services, dwindling cooperation with civil service. It was a situation which in the past had led to a breakdown of the economy and a change of dynasty.

Bustamonte cracked his knuckles nervously as he considered his position. At the moment he was committed to a course of action. The Medallion must die, and likewise the Breakness Wizard.

Daylight had come; now they could properly be executed.

He descended to the main floor, signaled to one of the Mamarone. "Summon Captain Mornune."

Several minutes passed. The neutralioid returned.

"Where is Mornune?" demanded Bustamonte.

"Captain Mornune and two of the platoon have departed Pergolai."

Bustamonte wheeled around, dumbfounded. "Departed Pergolai?"

"This is my information."

Bustamonte glared at the guard, then looked toward the tower. "Come along!" He charged for the lift; the two were whisked high. Bustamonte marched down the corridor, to the confinement chamber. He peered through the spy-hole, looked all around the room. Then he furiously slid aside the door, crossed to the open window.

"It is all clear now," he ranted. "Beran is gone. The Dominie is gone. Both are fled to Eiljanre. There will be trouble."

He went to the window, stood looking out

into the distance. Finally he turned. "Your name is Andrade?"

"Hessenden Andrade."

"You are now Captain Andrade, in the place of Mornune."

"Very well."

"We return to Eiljanre. Make the necessary arrangements."

Bustamonte descended to the terrace, seated himself with a glass of brandy. Palafox clearly intended Beran to become Panarch. The Paonese loved a young Panarch and demanded the smooth progression of the dynasty; anything else disturbed their need for timeless continuity. Beran need only appear at Eiljanre, to be led triumphantly to the Great Palace, and arrayed in Utter Black.

Bustamonte took a great gulp of brandy. Well then, he had failed. Aiello was dead. Bustamonte could never demonstrate that Beran's hand had placed the fatal sting. Indeed, had not three Mercantil traders been executed for the very crime?

What to do? Actually, he could only proceed to Eiljanre and hope to establish himself as Ayudor-Senior, regent for Beran. Unless guided too firmly by Palafox, Beran would probably overlook his imprisonment; and if Palafox were intransigent, there were ways of dealing with him.

Bustamonte rose to his feet. Back to Eiljanre,

there to eat humble-pie; he had spent many years playing sycophant to Aiello, and the experience would stand him in good stead.

In the hours and days that followed, Bustamonte encountered three surprises of increasing magnitude.

The first was the discovery that neither Palafox nor Beran had arrived at Eiljanre, nor did they appear elsewhere on Pao. Bustamonte, at first cautious and tentative, began to breathe easier. Had the pair met with some unforeseen disaster? Had Palafox kidnapped the Medallion for reasons of his own?

The doubt was unsettling. Until he was assured of Beran's death he could not properly enjoy the perquisites of the Panarch's office. Likewise, the doubt had infected the vast Paonese masses. Daily their recalcitrance increased; Bustamonte's informers reported that everywhere he was known as Bustamonte Bereglo. "Bereglo" was a word typically Paonese, applied to an unskillful slaughter-house worker, or a creature which worries and gnaws its victim.

Bustamonte seethed inwardly, but comforted himself with outward rectitude, hoping either that the population would accept him as Panarch or that Beran would appear to give the lie to rumors, and submit to a more definite assassination.

Then came the second unsettling shock.

The Mercantil Ambassador delivered Bustamonte a statement which first excoriated the
Paonese government for the summary execution of the three trade attachés, broke off all
trade relations until indemnification was paid,
and set forth the required indemnification—a
sum which seemed ridiculously large to a
Paonese ruler, who every day in the course of
his duties might ordain death for a hundred
thousand persons.

Bustamonte had been hoping to negotiate a
new armament contract. As he had advised
Aiello, he offered a premium for sole rights to
the most advanced weapons. The note from
the Mercantil Ambassador destroyed all hope
of a new agreement.

The third shock was the most devastating
of all, and indeed reduced the first two to the
proportion of incidents.

The Brumbo Clan of Batmarsh, elevated to
primacy over a score of restless competitors,
needed a glory-earning coup to cement its position. Eban Buzbek, Hetman of the Brumbos,
therefore gathered a hundred ships, loaded
them with warriors and set forth against the
great world of Pao.

Perhaps he had only intended a foray: a
landing, a vast orgiastic assault, a quick garnering of booty, and departure—but passing
the outer ring of monitors he met only token
resistance, and landing on Vidamand, the most

disaffected continent, none at all. This was success of the wildest description!

Eban Buzbek took his ten thousand men to Donaspara, first city of Shraimand; and there was no one to dispute him. Six days after he landed on Pao he entered Eiljanre. The populace watched him and his glory-flushed army with sullen eyes; none made any resistance, even when their property was taken and their women violated. Warfare—even hit-and-run guerilla tactics—was not in the Paonese character.

VI

BERAN, MEDALLION and son of Panarch Aiello, had lived his life under the most uneventful circumstances. With his diet carefully prescribed and scheduled, he never had known hunger and so had never enjoyed food. His play was supervised by a corps of trained gymnasts and was considered "exercise"; consequently he had no inclination for games. His person was tended and groomed; every obstacle and danger was whisked from his path; he had never faced a challenge, and had never known triumph.

Sitting on Palafox's shoulders, stepping out through the window into the night, Beran felt as if he were living a nightmare. A sudden weightlessness—they were falling! His stomach contracted; the breath rose in his throat. He squirmed and cried out in fear. Falling, falling, falling, when would they strike?

"Quiet," said Palafox shortly.

Beran's eyes focused. He blinked. A lighted window moved past his vision. It passed below; they were not falling; they were rising! They were above the tower, above the pavilion! Up into the night they drifted, light as bubbles, up above the tower, up into the star-bright sky. Presently, Beran convinced himself that he was not dreaming; it was therefore through the magic of the Breakness wizard that they wafted through the middle-air, light as thistle-dowm. As his wonder grew, his fear lessened, and he peered into Palafox's face. "Where are we going?"

"Up to where I anchored my ship."

Beran looked wistfully down to the pavilion. It glowed in many colors, like a sea-anemone. He had no wish to return; there was only a vague regret. Up into the sky they floated, for fifteen quiet minutes, and the pavilion became a colored blot far below.

Palafox held out his left hand; impulses from the radarmesh in his palm were reflected back from the ground, converted into stimulus. High enough. Palafox touched his tongue to one of the plates in the tissue of his cheek, spoke a sharp syllable.

Moments passed; Palafox and Beran floated like wraiths. Then a long shape came to blot out the sky. Palafox reached, caught a hand-rail, swung himself and Beran along a hull to an entrance hatch. He pushed Beran into a staging chamber, followed and closed the hatch.

Interior lights glowed.

Beran, too dazed to take an interest in events, sagged upon a bench. He watched Palafox mount to a raised deck, flick at a pair of keys. The sky went dull, and Beran was caught in the pulse of sub-space motion.

Palafox came down from the platform, inspected Beran with dispassionate appraisal. Beran could not meet his gaze.

"Where are we going?" asked Beran, not because he cared, but because he could think of nothing better to say.

"To Breakness."

Beran's heart took a queer jump. "Why must I go?"

"Because now you are Panarch. If you remained on Pao, Bustamonte would kill you."

Beran recognized the truth of the statement. He stole a look at Palafox—a man far different from the quiet stranger at Aiello's table. This Palafox was tall as a firedemon, magnificent with pent energy. A wizard, a Breakness wizard!

Palafox glanced down at Beran. "How old are you, boy?"

"Nine years old."

Palafox rubbed his long chin. "It is best that you learn what is to be expected of you. In essense, the program is uncomplicated. You

will live on Breakness, you shall attend the
Institute, you shall be my ward, and the time
will come when you serve me as one of my
own sons."

"Are your sons my age?" Beran asked hopefully.

"I have many sons!" said Palafox with grim
pride. "I count them by the hundreds!" Becoming aware of Beran's bemused attention,
he laughed humorlessly. "There is much here
that you do not understand. . . . Why do you
stare?"

Beran said apologetically, "If you have so
many children you must be old, much older
than you look."

Palafox's face underwent a peculiar change.
The cheeks suffused with red, his eyes glittered like bits of glass. His voice was slow, icy
cold. "I am not old. Never make such a remark again. It is an ill thing to say to a
Breakness dominie!"

"I'm sorry!" quavered Beran. "I thought . . ."

"No matter. Come, you are tired, you shall
sleep."

Beran awoke in puzzlement to find himself
not in his pink and black bed. After contemplating his position, he felt relatively cheer-
ful. The future promised to be interesting, and
when he returned to Pao he would be equipped
with all the secret lore of Breakness.

He rose from the bunk, shared breakfast with Palafox, who seemed to be in high spirits. Beran took sufficient courage to put a few further inquries. "Are you actually a wizard?"

"I can perform no miracles," said Palafox, "except perhaps those of the mind."

"But you walk on air! You shoot fire from your finger."

"As does any other Breakness dominie."

Beran looked wonderingly at the long keen visage. "Then you are all wizards?"

"Bah!" exclaimed Palafox. "These powers are the result of bodily modification. I am highly modified."

Beran's awe became tinged with doubt. "The Mamarone are modified, but . . ."

Palafox grinned down at Beran like a wolf. "This is the least apt comparison. Can neutraloids walk on air?"

"No."

"We are not neutraloids," said Palafox decisively. "Our modifications enhance rather than eliminate our powers. Antigravity web is meshed into the skin of my feet. Radar in my left hand, at the back of my neck, in my forehead, provides me with a sixth sense. I can see three colors below the red and four over the violet. I can hear radio waves. I can walk under water; I can float in space. Instead of bone in my forefinger, I carry a projection tube. I have a number of other powers, all drawing energy from a pack fitted into my chest."

Beran was silent for a moment. Then he asked diffidently, "When I come to Breakness, will I be modified too?"

Palafox considered Beran as if in the light of a new idea. "If you do exactly as I say you must do."

Beran turned his head. "What must I do?"

"For the present, you need not concern yourself."

Beran went to the port and looked out, but nothing could be seen but speed-striations of gray and black.

"How long before we reach Breakness?" he asked.

"Not so very long. . . . Come away from the port. Looking into sub-space can harm a susceptible brain."

Indicators on the control panel vibrated and fluttered; the space-boat gave a quick lurch.

Palafox stepped up to look from the observation dome. "Here is Breakness!"

Beran, standing on his tiptoes, saw a gray world, and behind, a small white sun. The space-boat whistled down into the atmosphere, and the world grew large.

Beran glimpsed mountains enormous beyond imagination: claws of rock forty miles high trailing plumes of vapor, rimed by ice and snow. The boat slipped across a gray-green ocean, mottled by clumps of floating weed, then once more rode over the crags.

The boat, now moving slowly, dipped into a vast valley with rock-slab walls and a bottom hidden by haze and murk. Ahead, a rocky slope, wide as a prairie, showed a trifle of gray-white crust. The boat approached, and the crust became a small city clinging to the shoulder of the mountain-side. The buildings were low, constructed of rock-melt with roofs of russet brown; some of them joined and hung down the crag like a chain. The effect was bleak and not at all imposing.

"Is that Breakness?" asked Beran.

"That is Breakness Institute," said Palafox.

Beran was vaguely disappointed. "I had expected something different."

"We make no pretensions," Palafox remarked. "There are, after all, a very few dominie. And we see very little of each other."

Beran started to speak, then hesitated, sensing that he was touching upon a sensitive subject. In a cautious voice he asked, "Do your sons all live with you?"

"No," said Palafox shortly. "They attend the Institute, naturally."

The boat sank slowly; the indicators on the control board fluttered and jumped as if alive.

Beran, looking across the chasm, remembered the verdant landscape and blue seas of his homeland with a pang. "When will I go back to Pao?" he asked in sudden anxiety.

Palafox, his mind on other matters, answered offhandedly. "As soon as conditions warrant."

"But when will that be?"

Palafox looked swiftly down at him. "Do you want to be Panarch of Pao?"

"Yes," said Beran decidedly. "If I could be modified."

"Perhaps you may be granted these wishes. But you must never forget that he who gets must give."

"What must I give?"

"We will discuss this matter later."

"Bustamonte will not welcome me," said Beran gloomily. "I think he wants to be Panarch, too."

Palafox laughed. "Bustamonte is having his troubles. Rejoice that Bustamonte must cope with them and not you."

VII

BUSTAMONTE'S TROUBLES were large. His dreams of grandeur were exploded. Instead of ruling the eight continents of Pao and holding court at Eiljanre, his retinue consisted of a dozen Mamarone, three of his least desirable concubines, and a dozen disgruntled officials of magisterial rank. His realm was a remote village on the rain-swept moors of Nonamand; his palace a tavern. He enjoyed these prerogatives only on the sufferance of the Brumbos who, enjoying the fruits of their conquest, felt no great urge to seek out and destroy Bustamonte.

A month passed. Bustamonte's temper grew short. He beat the concubines, berated his followers. The shepherds of the region took to avoiding the village; the innkeeper and the villagers every day became more taciturn, until one morning Bustamonte awoke to find the village deserted, the moors desolate of flocks.

Bustamonte dispatched half the neutraloids to forage for food, but they never returned. The ministers openly made plans to return to a more hospitable environment. Bustamonte argued and promised, but the Paonese mind was not easily amenable to any sort of persuasion.

Early one dreary morning the remaining neutraloids decamped. The concubines refused to bestir themselves, but sat huddled together, sniffling with head cold. All forenoon a miserable rain fell; the tavern became dank. Bustamonte ordered Est Coelho, Minister of Inter-Continental Transport, to arrange a blaze in the fireplace, but Coelho was in no mood to truckle to Bustamonte. Tempers seethed, boiled over; as a result, the entire group of ministers marched forth into the rain and set out for the coastal port of Spyrianthe.

The three women stirred, looked after the ministers, then like a single creature, turned to look slyly toward Bustamonte. He was alert. At the expression on his face, they sighed and groaned.

Cursing and panting, Bustamonte broke up the tavern furniture and built a roaring blaze in the fireplace.

There was a sound from outside, a faint chorus of yells, a wild *"Rip-rip-rip!"*

Bustamonte's heart sank, his jaw sagged. This was the hunting chivvy of the Brumbos, the clan call.

The yelling and *rip-rip-rip!* grew keener, and finally came down the single street of the village.

Bustamonte wrapped a cloak about his stocky frame, went to the door, flung it open, stepped out upon the cobbles.

Down the road from the moors came his ministers at a staggering lope. Above, a dozen warriors of the Brumbo Clan rode air-horses, cavorting, whooping and shouting, herding the ministers like sheep. At the sight of Bustamonte they screamed in triumph, swung down, grounded their air-horses, sprang forward, each anxious to be first to lay hands on the nape of Bustamonte's neck.

Bustamonte retreated into the doorway, resolved to die with dignity intact. He bought out his wasp, and blood would have flowed had not the Batch warriors stood back.

Down flew Eban Buzbek himself, a wiry jug-eared little man, his yellow hair plaited into a foot-long queue. The keel of his air-horse clattered along the cobbles; the tubes sighed and sputtered.

Eban Buzbek marched forward, pushed through the sobbing huddle of ministers, reached to seize Bustamonte by the nape and force him to his knees. Bustamonte backed further into the doorway, pointed his wasp. But the Brumbo warriors were quick; their shock-pistols bellowed and Bustamonte was buffeted against the wall. Eban Buzbek seized him by the neck and hurled him into the mud of the street.

Bustamonte slowly picked himself up to stand shaking in rage.

Eban Buzbek waved his hand. Bustamonte was seized, trussed with belts, rolled into a net. Without further ado, the Brumbos climbed into the saddles and rode through the sky, with Bustamonte hanging below like a pig for the market.

At Spyrianthe, the group transferred into a domed airship. Bustamonte, dazed from the buffeting wind, half-dead of chill, slipped to the deck, and knew nothing of the trip back to Eiljanre.

The air-ship landed in the court of the Grand Palace; Bustamonte was hustled through the ravaged halls and locked in a sleeping-chamber.

Early the next day, two women servants roused him. They cleaned him of mud and grime, dressed him in clean clothes, brought him food and drink.

An hour later the door opened; a clansman signaled. Bustamonte came forth, pallid, nervous but still uncowed.

He was taken to a morning room overlooking the famous palace florarium. Here Eban

Buzbek waited with a group of his clansman and a Mercantil interpreter. He seemed in the best of spirits, and nodded jovially when Bustamonte appeared. He spoke a few words in the staccato language of Batmarsh; the Mercantil translated.

"Eban Buzbek hopes you have passed a restful night."

"What does he want of me?" growled Bustamonte.

The message was translated. Eban Buzbek replied at considerable length. The Mercantil listened attentively, then turned to Bustamonte.

"Eban Buzbek returns to Batmarsh. He says the Paonese are sullen and stubborn. They refuse to cooperate as a defeated people should."

The news came as no surprise to Bustamonte.

"Eban Buzbek is disappointed in Pao. He says the people are turtles, in that they will neither fight nor obey. He takes no satisfaction in his conquest."

Bustamonte glowered at the pig-tailed clansman slouching in the Black chair.

"Eban Buzbek departs and leaves you as Panarch of Pao. For this favor you must pay one million marks each Paonese month for the duration of your reign. Do you agree to the arrangement?"

Bustamonte looked from face to face. No one looked at him directly; the expressions were empty. But each warrior seemed peculiarly taut, like runners crouched at the start of a race.

"Do you agree to the arrangement?" the Mercantil repeated.

"Yes," muttered Bustamonte.

The Mercantil translated. Eban Buzbek made a sign of assent, rose to his feet. A piper bent to his diplonet, blew a brisk march. Eban Buzbek and his warriors departed the hall without so much as a glance for Bustamonte.

An hour later, Buzbek's red and black corvette knifed up and away; before the day's end no single clansman remained on Pao.

With a tremendous effort Bustamonte asserted his dignity, and assumed the title and authority of Panarch. His fifteen billion subjects, diverted by the Batch invasion, showed no further recalcitrance; and in this respect, Bustamonte profited from the incursion.

VIII

BERAN'S FIRST WEEKS on Breakness were dismal and unhappy. There was no variety, inside or out; all was rock-color, in varying tones and intensities, and the look of distance. The wind roared incessantly, but air was thin, and the effort of breathing left an acid burn in Beran's throat. Like a small pale house-sprite, he wandered the chilly corridors of Palafox's mansion, hoping for diversion, finding little.

The typical residence of a Breakness Dominie, Palafox's house hung down the slope on the spine of an escalator. At the top were workrooms not permitted to Beran, but where he glimpsed marvelously intricate mechanisms. Below were rooms of general function paneled in dark board, with floors of russet rock-melt, generally unoccupied except for Beran. At the bottom, separated from the main chain of rooms, was a large circular structure, which

Beran eventually discovered to be Palafox's private dormitory.

The house was austere and chilly, without devices of amusement or ornament. No one heeded Beran; it was as if his very existence were forgotten. He ate from a buffet in the central hall, he slept where and when it suited him. He learned to recognize half a dozen men who seemed to make Palafox's house their headquarters. Once or twice in the lower part of the house he glimpsed a woman. No one spoke to him except Palafox, but Beran saw him only rarely.

On Pao there was small distinction between the sexes; both wore similar garments and enjoyed identical privileges. Here the differences were emphasized. Men wore dark suits of close-fitting fabric and black skull-caps with pointed bills. Those women whom Beran had glimpsed wore flouncing skirts of gay colors— the only color to be seen on Breakness—tight vests which left the midriff uncovered, slippers tinkling with bells. Their heads were uncovered, their hair was artfully dressed; all were young and handsome.

When he could tolerate the house no longer, Beran bundled himself into warm garments and ventured out on the mountainside. He bent his head into the wind and pushed to the east until he reached the verge of the settlement, where the Wind River dwindled in mighty perspective. A mile below were a half-dozen large structures: automatic fabrication plants. Above reared the rock slope, far up to the gray sky, where the wild little white sun swerved like a tin disc on the wind. Beran retraced his steps.

A week later he ventured forth again, and this time turned west with the wind at his back. A lane melted from the rock wound and twisted among dozens of long houses like that of Palafox, and other lanes veered off at angles, until Beran became concerned lest he lose his way.

He halted within sight of Breakness Institute, a group of bleak buildings stepped down the slope. They were several stories high, taller than other buildings of the settlement, and received the full force of the wind. Streaks of sooty gray and black-green ran across the gray rock-melt, where years of driven rime and sleet had left their marks.

As he stood, a group of boys several years older than himself came up the road from the Institute; they swerved up the hill, marching in a solemn line, apparently bound for the space-port.

Curious! thought Beran. How unsmiling and silent they seemed. Paonese lads would have been skipping and skylarking.

He found his way back to Palafox's manse,

puzzling over the lack of social intercourse on Breakness.

The novelty of life on the new planet had worn smooth; the pangs of homesickness stabbed Beran hard. He sat on the settee in the hall tying aimless knots in a bit of string. There was the sound of footsteps; Beran looked up. Palafox entered the hall, began to pass through, then noticed Beran and came to a halt. "Well, the young Panarch of Pao—why do you sit so quietly?"

"I have nothing to do."

Palafox nodded. The Paonese were not ones to undertake gratuitously any arduous intellectual program; and Palafox had intended that Beran should become utterly bored, to provide incentive for the task.

"Nothing to do?" inquired Palafox, as if surprised. "Well, we must remedy that." He appeared to cogitate. "If you are to attend the Institute, you must learn the language of Breakness."

Beran was suddenly aggrieved. "When do I go back to Pao?" he asked querulously.

Palafox shook his head solemnly. "I doubt if you'd wish to return at this moment."

"But I do!"

Palafox seated himself beside Beran. "Have you heard of the Brumbos of Batmarsh?"

"Batmarsh is a small planet three stars from Pao inhabited by quarrelsome people."

"Correct. The Batch are divided into twenty-three clans, which continually compete in valor. The Brumbos, who are one of these clans, have invaded Pao."

Beran heard the news without total comprehension. "Do you mean . . ."

"Pao is now the personal province of Eban Buzbek, Hetman of the Brumbos. Ten thousand clansmen in a few painted war-ships took all Pao, and your uncle Bustamonte lives in forlorn circumstances."

"What will happen now?"

Palafox laughed shortly. "Who knows? But it is best that you remain on Breakness. Your life would be worth nothing on Pao."

"I don't want to stay here. I don't like Breakness."

"No?" Palafox pretended surprise. "Why is that?"

"Everything is different from Pao. There isn't any sea, no trees, no . . ."

"Naturally!" exclaimed Palafox. "We have no trees, but we have Breakness Institute. Now you will start learning, and then you'll find Breakness more interesting. First, the language of Breakness! We start at once. Come!" He rose to his feet.

Beran's interest in the Breakness language

was minuscule, but activity of any kind would
be welcome—as Palafox had foreseen.

Palafox stalked to the escalator, with Beran
behind; they rode to the top of the house—
rooms heretofore barred to Beran—and entered
a wide workshop exposed to the gray-white
sky through a ceiling of glass. A young man in
a skintight suit of dark brown, one of Palafox's
many sons, looked up from his work. He was
thin and taut, his features hard and bold. He
resembled Palafox to a marked degree, even
to tricks of gesture and poise of head. Palafox
could take pride in such evidence of genetic
vigor, which tended to shape all of his sons
into near-simulacra of himself. On Breakness,
status was based on a quality best described
as the forcible imprinting of self upon the
future.

Between Palafox and Fanchiel, the young
man in the dark brown suit, neither empathy
nor hostility evinced itself openly: indeed the
emotion was so all-pervasive throughout the
houses, dormitories, and hall of the Institute
as to be taken for granted.

Fanchiel had been tinkering with a minute
fragment of mechanism clamped in a vise. He
watched a magnified three-dimensional image of the device on a stage at eye level; he
wore gauntlets controlling micro-tools, and
easily manipulated components invisible to

the naked eye. At the sight of Palafox, he rose from his work, subordinating himself to the more intense ego of his progenitor.

The two men spoke in the language of Breakness for several minutes. Beran began to hope that he had been forgotten—then Palafox snapped his fingers. "This is Fanchiel, thirty-third of my sons. He will teach you much that is useful. I urge you to industry, enthusiasm and application—not after the Paonese fashion, but like the student at Breakness Institute, which we hope you shall become." He departed without further words.

Fanchiel unenthusiastically put aside his work. "Come," he said in Paonese, and led the way into an adjoining room.

"First—a preliminary discussion." He pointed to a desk of gray metal with a black rubber top. "Sit there, if you please."

Beran obeyed. Fanchiel appraised him carefully, without regard for Beran's sensibilities. Then, with the faintest of shrugs, he dropped his own taut-muscled body into a chair.

"Our first concern," he said, "will be the language of Breakness."

Accumulated resentments suddenly merged inside Beran: the neglect, the boredom, the homesickness, and now this last cavalier disregard for his personal individuality. "I don't care to learn Breakness. I want to return to Pao."

Fanchiel seemed vaguely amused. "In time you certainly will return to Pao—perhaps as Panarch. If you returned at this moment you would be killed."

Beran's eyes stung with loneliness and misery. "When can I go back?"

"I don't know," said Fanchiel. "Lord Palafox is undertaking some great plan in connection with Pao—you will undoubtedly return when he thinks best. In the meanwhile, you would do well to accept such advantages as are offered you."

Beran's reason and native willingness to oblige struggled with the obstinacy of his race. "Why must I go to the Institute?"

Fanchiel replied with ingenuous candor. "Lord Palafox apparently intends that you should identify with Breakness and so feel sympathetic to his goals."

Beran could not grasp this; however, he was impressed by Fanchiel's manner. "What will I learn at the Institute?"

"A thousand things—more than I can describe to you. In the College of Comparative Culture—where Lord Palafox is Dominie—you will study the races of the universe, their similarities and differences, their languages and basic urges, the specific symbols by which you can influence them.

"In the College of Mathematics you learn the manipulation of abstract ideas, various systems of rationality—likewise you are trained to make quick mental calculations.

"In the College of Human Anatomy you learn geriatry and death prevention, pharmacology, the technique of human modification and augmentation—and possibly you will be allowed one or two modifications."

Beran's imagination was stimulated. "Could I be modified like Palafox?"

"Ha hah!" exclaimed Fanchiel. "This is an amusing idea. Are you aware that Lord Palafox is one of the most powerfully modified men of Breakness? He controls nine sensitivities, four energies, three projections, two nullifications, three lethal emanations, in addition to miscellaneous powers such as the mental slide-rule, the ability to survive in a de-oxygenated atmosphere, anti-fatigue glands, a sub-clavicle blood chamber which automatically counteracts any poison he may have ingested. No, my ambitious young friend!" For an instant the jutting features became soft with amusement. "But if ever you rule Pao, you will control a worldful of fecund girls, and thus you may command every modification known to the surgeons and anatomists of Breakness Institute."

Beran looked blankly at Fanchiel, quite at a loss. Modification, even under these incomprehensible but questionable terms, seemed a long way in the future.

"Now," said Fanchiel briskly, "to the language of Breakness."

With the prospect of modification removed to the far future, Beran's obstinacy returned. "Why can't we speak Paonese?"

Fanchiel explained patiently. "You will be required to learn a great deal that you could not understand if I taught Paonese."

"I understand you now," muttered Beran.

"Because we are discussing the most general ideas. Each language is a special tool, with a particular capability. It is more than a means of communication, it is a system of thought. Do you understand what I mean?"

Fanchiel found his answer in Beran's expression.

"Think of a language as the contour of a watershed, stopping flow in certain directions, channeling it into others. Language controls the mechanism of your mind. When people speak different languages, their minds work differently and they act differently. For instance: you know of the planet Vale?"

"Yes. The world where all the people are insane."

"Better to say, their actions give the impression of insanity. Actually they are complete anarchists. Now if we examine the speech of Vale we find, if not a reason for the behavior, at least a parallelism. Language on Vale is personal improvisation, with the fewest possible conventions. Each individual selects a speech as you or I might choose the color of our garments."

Beran frowned. "We Paonese are not careless in such matters. Our dress is established, and no one would wear a costume unfamiliar to him, or one which right cause misunderstanding."

A smile broke the austere cast of Fanchiel's face. "True, true; I forgot. The Paonese make no virtue of conspicuous dress. And—possibly as a corollary—mental abnormality is rare. The Paonese, fifteen billion of them, are pleasantly sane. Not so the people of Vale. They live to complete spontaneity—in clothes, in conduct, in language. The question arises: does the language provoke or merely reflect the eccentricity? Which came first: the language or the conduct?"

Beran admitted himself at a loss.

"In any event," said Fanchiel, "now that you have been shown the connection between language and conduct, you will be anxious to learn the language of Breakness."

Beran was unflatteringly dubious. "Would I then become like you?"

Fanchiel asked sardonically, "A fate to be avoided at all costs? I can relieve your anxiety. All of us change as we learn, but you can never become a true man of Breakness. Long ago you were shaped into the Paonese style.

But speaking our language, you will understand us—and if you can think as another man thinks, you cannot dislike him. Now, if you are ready, we commence."

IX

On Pao there was peace and the easy flow of life. The population tilled their farms, fished the oceans, and in certain districts sieved great wads of pollen from the air, to make a pleasant honey-tasting cake. Every eighth day was market day; on the eight-times-eighth day, the people gathered for the drones; on the eight-times-eight-times eighth day, occurred the continental fairs.

The people had abandoned all opposition to Bustamonte. Defeat at the hands of the Brumbos was forgotten; Bustamonte's taxes were easier than those of Aiello and he ruled with a lack of ostentation befitting his ambiguous accession to the Black.

But Bustamonte's satisfaction at the attainment of his ambition was not complete. He was by no means a coward, but personal safety became an obsession; a dozen casual visitors

who chanced to make abrupt motions were
exploded by Mamarone hammer-guns. Bustamonte likewise imagined himself the subject
of contemptuous jest, and other dozens lost
their lives for displaying a merry expression
when Bustamonte's eye happened to fall upon
them. The bitterest circumstance of all was
the tribute to Eban Buzbek, Hetman of the
Brumbos.

Each month Bustamonte framed a stinging
defiance to send Eban Buzbek in lieu of the
million marks, but each month caution pre-
vailed; Bustamonte, in helpless rage, dispatched the tribute.

Four years passed; then one morning a red,
black and yellow courier ship arrived at the
Eiljanre spaceport, to discharge Cormoran
Benbarth, scion of a junior branch of the
Buzbeks. He presented himself at the Grand
Palace as an absentee landlord might visit an
outlying farm and greeted Bustamonte with
casual amiability.

Bustamonte, wearing the Utter Black, maintained an expressionless face with great effort. He made the ceremonial inquiry: "What
fortunate wind casts you upon our shores?"

Cormoran Benbarth, a tall young bravo with
braided blond hair and magnificent blond mustaches, studied Bustamonte through eyes blue
as cornflowers, wide and innocent as the
Paonese sky.

"My mission is simple," he said. "I have come into possession of the North Faden Barony, which as you may or may not know is hard against the south countries of the Griffin Clan. I require funds for fortification and recruitment of followers."

"Ah," said Bustamonte. Cormoran Benbarth tugged at the drooping blond mustache.

"Eban Buzbek suggested that you might spare a million marks from your plenty, in order to incur my gratitude."

Bustamonte sat like an image of stone. His eyes held the innocent blue gaze for thirty seconds while his mind raced furiously. It was inconceivable that the request could be anything other than a demand backed by an implicit threat of violence, to which he could offer no resistance. He threw up his arms in frustration, ordered forth the required sum and received Cormoran Benbarth's thanks in baleful silence.

Benbarth returned to Batmarsh in a mood of mild gratitude; Bustamonte's fury induced an abdominal acerbation. It presently became clear that he must swallow his pride and petition those whose offices he had once rejected: the dominies of Breakness Institute.

Assuming the identity of an itinerant engineer, Bustamonte took passage to the depot planet Journal and there boarded a packet for the voyage through the outer Marklaides. Presently he arrived at Breakness.

A lighter came up to meet the packet. Bustamonte gratefully departed the cramped hull, and was conveyed down through gigantic crags to the Institute.

At the terminus, he encountered none of the formalities which gave occupation to a numerous branch of the Paonese civil service; in fact he was given no notice whatever.

Bustamonte became vexed. He went to the portal, looked down across the city. To the left were factories and workshops, to the right the austere mass of the Institute, in between the various houses, manors and lodges, each with its appended dormitory.

A stern-faced young man—hardly more than a lad—tapped him on the arm, motioned him to the side. Bustamonte stepped back as a draft of twenty young women with hair pale as cream moved past him. They entered a scarab-shaped car, which slid away down-slope.

No other vehicle could be seen, and the terminal was now almost empty. Bustamonte, white with anger, the knobs of muscles twitching in his cheeks, at last admitted that either he was not expected, or that no one had thought to meet him. It was intolerable! He would command attention; it was his due!

He strode to the center of the terminus, and made imperious motions. One or two persons paused curiously, but when he commanded them in Paonese to fetch a responsible authority, they looked at him blankly and continued on their way.

Bustamonte ceased his efforts; the terminus was vacant except for himself. He recited one of the rolling Paonese curses, and went once more to the portal.

The settlement was naturally unfamiliar; the nearest house was a half-mile distant. Bustamonte glanced in alarm toward the sky. The little white sun had fallen behind a crag; a murky fog was flowing down Wind River; light was failing over the settlement.

Bustamonte heaved a deep breath. There was no help for it; the Panarch of Pao must tramp his way to shelter like a vagabond. Grimly he pushed open the door, and stepped forth.

The wind caught him, wheeled him down the lane; the cold ate through his thin Paonese garments. He turned, ran on his short thick legs down the lane.

Chilled to the bone, his lungs aching, he arrived at the first house. The rock-melt walls rose above him, bare of opening. He trudged along the face of the building, but could find no entrance; and so crying out in anguish and rage, he continued down the road.

The sky was dark; small pellets of sleet began to sting the back of his neck. He ran to another house, and this time found a door, but no one responded to his pounding. He turned away, shivering and shaking, feet numb, fingers aching. The gloom was now so thick he could barely distinguish the way.

Lights shone from windows of the third house; again no one responded to his pounding at the door. In fury Bustamonte seized a rock, threw it at the nearest window. The glass clanged: a satisfying noise. Bustamonte threw another rock, and at last attracted attention. The door opened; Bustamonte fell inside stiff as a toppling tree.

The young man caught him, dragged him to a seat. Bustamonte sat rigid, feet sprawled, eyes bulging, breath coming in sobs.

The man spoke; Bustamonte could not understand. "I am Bustamonte, Panarch of Pao," he said, the words coming blurred and fuzzy through his stiff lips. "This is an ill reception— someone shall pay dearly."

The young man, a son of the resident Dominie, had no acquaintance with Paonese. He shook his head, and seemed rather bored. He looked toward the door and back to Bustamonte, as if preparing to eject the unintelligible intruder.

"I am Panarch of Pao!" screamed Bustamonte. "Take me to Palafox, Lord Palafox, do you hear? Palafox!"

The name evoked a response. The man signaled Bustamonte to remain in his seat and disappeared into another room.

Ten minutes passed. The door opened, Palafox appeared. He bowed with bland punctilio. "Ayudor Bustamonte, it is a pleasure to see you. I was unable to meet you at the terminal, but I see that you have managed very well. My house is close at hand, and I would be pleased to offer you hospitality. Are you ready?"

The next morning Bustamonte took a tight check-rein on himself. Indignation could accomplish nothing, and might place him at embarrassing odds with his host, although—he looked contemptuously around the room—the hospitality was poor quality indeed. Why would men so knowledgeable build with such austerity? In point in fact, why would they inhabit so harsh a planet?

Palafox presented himself, and the two sat down to a table with a carafe of peppery tea between them. Palafox confined himself to bland platitudes. He ignored the unpleasantness of their first meeting on Pao, and showed no interest in the reason for Bustamonte's presence.

At last Bustamonte hitched himself forward and spoke to the point. "The late Panarch

Aiello at one time sought your aid. He acted, as I see now, with foresight and wisdom. Therefore I have come in secrecy to Breakness to arrange a new contract between us."

Palafox nodded, sipping his tea without comment.

"The situation is this," said Bustamonte. "The accursed Brumbos exact a monthly tribute from me. I pay without pleasure—nevertheless I make no great complaint, for it comes cheaper than maintaining arms against them."

"The worst loser appears to be Mercantil," observed Palafox.

"Exactly!" said Bustamonte. "Recently, however, an additional extortion occurred. I fear it to be the forerunner of many more similar." Bustamonte described the visit of Cormoran Benbarth. "My treasury will be open to endless forays—I will become no more than paymaster for all the bravos of Batmarsh. I refuse to submit to this ignoble subservience! I will free Pao: this is my mission! For this reason I come for counsel and strategic advice."

Palafox arranged his goblet of tea with a delicacy conveying an entire paragraph of meaning. "Advice is our only export. It is yours—at a price."

"And this price?" asked Bustamonte, though he well knew.

Palafox settled himself more comfortably in his chair. "As you know, this is a world of men, and so has been since the founding of the Institute. But necessarily we persist, we sire offspring, we rear our sons—those whom we deem worthy of us. It is the lucky child who wins admission to Breakness Institute. For each of these, twenty depart the planet with their mothers, when the indenture expires."

"In short," said Bustamonte crisply, "you want women." .

Palafox nodded. "We want women—healthy young women of intelligence and beauty. This is the only commodity which we wizards of Breakness cannot fabricate—nor would we care to."

"What of your own daughters?" Bustamonte asked curiously. "Can you not breed daughters as easily as sons?"

The words made no impression upon Palafox; it was almost as if he had not heard them. "Breakness is a world of men," he said. "We are Wizards of the Institute."

Bustamonte sat in pensive consideration unaware that to a man of Breakness, a daughter was scarcely more desirable than a two-headed Mongoloid. The Breakness dominie, like the classical ascetics, lived in the present, certain only of his own ego; the past was a record, the future an amorphous blot waiting for shape. He might lay plans for a hundred years ahead; for while the Breakness wizard paid lip-service to the inevitability of death, emotionally he rejected it, convinced that in the proliferation of sons he merged himself with the future.

Bustamonte, ignorant of Breakness psychology, was only reinforced in the conviction that Palafox was slightly mad. Reluctantly he said, "We can arrive at a satisfactory contract. For your part, you must join us in crushing the Batch, and ensuring that never again . . ."

Palafox smiling, shook his head. "We are not warriors. We sell the workings of our minds, no more. How can we dare otherwise? Breakness is vulnerable. A single missile could destroy the Institute. You will contract with me alone. If Eban Buzbek arrived here tomorrow he could buy counsel from another wizard, and the two of us would pit our skills."

"Hmmph," growled Bustamonte. "What guarantee have I that he will not do so?"

"None whatever. The policy of the Institute is passionless neutrality—the individual wizards, however, may work where they desire, the better to augment their dormitories."

Bustamonte fretfully drummed his fingers. "What can you do for me, if you cannot protect me from the Brumbos?"

Palafox meditated, eyelids half-closed, then said, "There are a number of methods to achieve the goal you desire. I can arrange the hire of mercenaires from Hallowmede, or Polensis, or Earth. Possibly I could stimulate

a coalition of Batch clans against the Brumbos.
We could so debase Paonese currency that the
tribute became valueless."

Bustamonte frowned. "I prefer methods more
forthright. I want you to supply us tools of
war. Then we may defend ourselves, and so
need be at no one's mercy."

Palafox raised his crooked black eyebrows.
"Strange to hear such dynamic proposals from
a Paonese."

"Why not?" demanded Bustamonte. "We are
not cowards."

A hint of impatience entered Palafox's voice.
"Ten thousand Brumbos overcame fifteen billion Paonese. Your people had weapons. But
no one considered resistance. They acquiesced
like grass-birds."

Bustamonte shook his head doggedly. "We
are men like other men. All we need is training."

"Training will never supply the desire to
fight."

Bustamonte scowled. "Then this desire must
be supplied!"

Palafox showed his teeth in a peculiar grin.
He pulled himself erect in his chair. "At last
we have touched the core of the matter."

Bustamonte glanced at him, puzzled by his
sudden intensity.

Palafox continued. "We must persuade the
amenable Paonese to become fighters. How
can we do this? Evidently they must change

their basic nature. They must discard passivity and easy adjustment to hardship. They must learn truculence and pride and competitiveness. Do you agree?"

Bustamonte hesitated. "You may be right."

"This is no overnight process, you understand. **A change of basic psychology is a formidable process.**"

Bustamonte was touched by suspicion. There was strain in Palafox's manner, an effort at casualness.

"If you wish an effective fighting force," said Palafox, "here is the only means to that end. There is no shortcut."

Bustamonte looked away, out over the Wind River. "You believe that this fighting force can be created?"

"Certainly."

"And how much time might be required?"

"Twenty years, more or less."

"Twenty years!"

Bustamonte was silent several minutes. "I must think this over." He jumped to his feet, strode back and forth shaking his hands as if they were wet.

Palafox said with a trace of asperity: "How can it be otherwise? If you want a fighting force you must first create fighting spirit. This is a cultural trait and cannot be inculcated overnight."

"Yes, yes," muttered Bustamonte. "I see that you are right, but I must think."

"Think also on a second matter," Palafox suggested. "Pao is vast and populous. There is scope not merely for an effective army, but also a vast industrial complex might be established. Why buy goods from Mercantil when you can produce them yourself?"

"How can all this be done?"

Palafox laughed. "That is where you must employ my special knowledge. I am Dominie of Comparative Culture at Breakness Institute."

"Nevertheless," said Bustamonte obstinately, "I still must know how you propose to bring about these changes—never forgetting that Paonese resist change more adamantly than the advent of death."

"Exactly," replied Palafox. "We must alter the mental framework of the Paonese people— a certain proportion of them, at least—which is most easily achieved by altering the language."

Bustamonte shook his head. "This process sounds indirect and precarious. I had hoped . . ."

Palafox interrupted incisively. "Words are tools. Language is a pattern, and defines the way the word-tools are used."

Bustamonte was eying Palafox sidelong. "How can this theory be applied practically? Do you have a definite detailed plan?"

Palafox inspected Bustamonte with scornful amusement. "For an affair of such magnitude? You expect miracles even a Breakness Wizard cannot perform. Perhaps you had best continue with the tribute to Eban Buzbek of Batmarsh."

Bustamonte was silent.

"I command basic principles," said Palafox presently. "I apply these abstractions to practical situations. This is the skeleton of the operation, which finally is fleshed over with detail."

Bustamonte still remained silent.

"One point I will make," said Palafox, "that such an operation can only be effectuated by a ruler of great power, one who will not be swayed by maudlin sentiment."

"I have that power," said Bustamonte. "I am as ruthless as circumstances require."

"This is what must be done. One of the Paonese continents—or any appropriate area—will be designated. The people of this area will be persuaded to the use of a new language. That is the extent of the effort. Presently they will produce warriors in profusion."

Bustamonte frowned skeptically. "Why not undertake a program of education and training in arms? To change the language is going far afield."

"You have not grasped the essential point," said Palafox. "Paonese is a passive, dispassionate language. It presents the world in two dimensions, without tension or contrast. A people speaking Paonese, theoretically, ought to be docile, passive, without strong personality development—in fact, exactly as the Paonese people are. The new language will be based on the contrast and comparison of strength, with a grammar simple and direct. To illustrate, consider the sentence, 'The farmer chops down a tree.' " (Literally rendered from the Paonese in which the two men spoke, the sentence was: "Farmer *in state of exertion;* axe *agency;* tree *in state of subjection to attack.*") "In the new language the sentence becomes: 'The farmer overcomes the inertia of the axe; the axe breaks asunder the resistance of tree.' Or perhaps: 'The farmer vanquishes the tree, using the weapon-instrument of the axe.' "

"Ah," said Bustamonte appreciatively.

"The syllabary will be rich in effort-producing gutturals and hard vowels. A number of key ideas will be synonymous; such as *pleasure* and *overcoming a resistance—relaxation* and *shame—out-worlder* and *rival.* Even the clans of Batmarsh will seem mild compared to the future Paonese military."

"Yes, yes," breathed Bustamonte. "I begin to understand."

"Another area might be set aside for the inculcation of another language," said Palafox offhandedly. "In this instance, the grammar will be extravagantly complicated but altogether consistent and logical. The vocables would be discrete but joined and fitted by elaborate rules of accordance. What is the result? When a group of people, impregnated with these stimuli, are presented with supplies and facilities, industrial development is inevitable.

"And should you plan to seek ex-planetary markets, a corps of salesmen and traders might be advisable. Theirs would be a symmetrical language with emphatic number-parsing, elaborate honorifics to teach hypocrisy, a vocabularly rich in homophones to facilitate ambiguity, a syntax of reflection, reinforcement and alternation to emphasize the analogous interchange of human affairs.

"All these languages will make use of semantic assistance. To the military segment, a 'successful man' will be synonymous with 'winner of a fierce contest.' To the industrialists, it will mean 'efficient fabricator.' To the traders, it equates with 'a person irresistibly persuasive.' Such influences will pervade each of the languages. Naturally they will not act with equal force upon each individual, but the mass action must be decisive."

"Marvelous!" cried Bustamonte, completely won over. "This is human engineering indeed!"

Palafox went to the window and looked across Wind River. He was faintly smiling and his black eyes, usually so black and hard, were softly unfocused. For a moment his real age—twice Bustamonte's and more—was apparent; but only for a moment, and when he swung about, his face was as emotionless as ever.

"You understand that I merely talk at random—I formulate ideas, so to speak. Truly massive planning must be accomplished: the various languages must be synthesized, their vocabularies formulated. Instructors to teach the languages must be recruited. I can rely on my own sons. Another group must be organized, or perhaps derived from the first group: an elite corps of coordinators trained to fluency in each of the languages. This corps will ultimately become a managerial corporation, to assist your present civil service."

Bustamonte blew out his cheeks. "Well . . . possibly. So far-reaching a function for this group seems unnecessary. Enough that we create a military force to smite Eban Buzbek and his bandits!"

Bustamonte jumped to his feet, marched back and forth in excitement. He stopped short, looked slyly toward Palafox. "One further point we must discuss: what will be the fee for your services?"

"Six brood of women a month," said Palafox calmly, "of optimum intelligence and physique, between the ages of fourteen and twenty-four years, their time of indenture not to exceed fifteen years, their transportation back to Pao guaranteed, together with all substandard and female offspring."

Bustamonte, with a knowing smile, shook his head. "Six brood—is this not excessive?"

Palafox darted him a burning glance. Bustamonte, aware of his mistake, added hastily, "However, I will agree to this figure. In return you must return me my beloved nephew, Beran, so that he may make preparation for a useful career."

"As a visitor to the floor of the sea?"

"We must take account of realities," murmured Bustamonte.

"I agree," said Palafox in a flat voice. "They dictate that Beran Panasper, Panarch of Pao, complete his education on Breakness."

Bustamonte broke out into furious protest; Palafox responded tartly. Palafox remained contemptuously calm, and Bustamonte at last acceded to his terms.

The bargain was recorded upon film and the two parted, if not amicably, at least in common accord.

X

WINTER ON BREAKNESS was a time of chill, of thin clouds flying down Wind River, of hail fine as sand hissing along the rock. The sun careened only briefly above the vast rock slab to the south, and for most of the day Breakness Institute was shrouded in murk.

Five times the dismal season came and passed, and Beran Panasper acquired a basic Breakness education.

The first two years Beran lived in the house of Palafox, and much of his energy was given to learning the language. His natural preconceptions regarding the function of speech were useless, for the language of Breakness was different from Paonese in many significant respects. Paonese was of that type known as "polysynthetic," with root words taking on prefixes, affixes and postpositions to extend their meaning. The language of Breakness was basically "isolative," but unique in that it derived entirely from the speaker: that is to say, the speaker was the frame of reference upon which the syntax depended, a system which made for both logical elegance and simplicity. Since Self was the implicit basis of expression, the pronoun "I" was unnecessary. Other personal pronouns were likewise non-existent, except for third person constructions—although these actually were contractions of noun phrases.

The language included no negativity; instead there were numerous polarities such as "go" and "stay." There was no passive voice—every verbal idea was self-contained: "to strike," "to receive-impact." The language was rich in words for intellectual manipulation, but almost totally deficient in descriptives of various emotional states. Even if a Breakness dominie chose to break his solipsistic shell and reveal his mood, he would be forced to the use of clumsy circumlocution.

Such common Paonese concepts as "anger," "joy," "love," "grief," were absent from the Breakness vocabulary. On the other hand, there were words to define a hundred different types of ratiocination, subtleties unknown to the Paonese—distinctions which baffled Beran so completely that at times his entire stasis, the solidity of his ego, seemed threatened. Week after week Fanchiel explained, illustrated, paraphrased; little by little Beran assimilated the unfamiliar mode of thought—and, simultaneously, the Breakness approach to existence.

Then ... one day Palafox summoned him and remarked that Beran's knowledge of the language was adequate for study at the Institute; that he would immediately be enrolled for the basic regimen.

Beran felt hollow and forlorn. The house of Palafox had provided a certain melancholy security; what would he find at the Institute?

Palafox dismissed him, and half an hour later Fanchiel escorted him to the great rock-melt quadrangle, saw him enrolled and installed in a cubicle at the student dormitory. He then departed, and Beran henceforth saw nothing either of Fanchiel or of Palafox.

So began a new phrase of Beran's existence on Breakness. All his previous education had been conducted by tutors; he had participated in none of the vast Paonese recitatives, wherein thousands of children chanted in unison all their learning—the youngest piping the numbers "Ai! Shrai! Vida! Mina! Nona! Drona! Hivan! Imple!"; the oldest the epic drones with which Paonese erudition concerned itself. For this reason Beran was not as puzzled by the customs of the Institution as he might have been.

Each youth was recognized as an individual, as singular and remote as a star in space.

He lived by himself, shared no officially recognized phase of his existence with any other student. When spontaneous conversations occurred, the object was to bring an original viewpoint, or novel sidelight, to the discussion at hand. The more unorthodox the idea, the more certain that it would at once be attacked. He who presented it must then defend his idea to the limits of logic, but not beyond. If successful, he gained prestige; if routed, he was accordingly diminished.

Another subject enjoyed a furtive currency among the students: the subject of age and death. The topic was more or less taboo—especially in the presence of a dominie—for no one died of disease or corporeal degeneration on Breakness. The dominies ranged the universe; a certain number met violent ends in spite of their built-in weapons and defenses. The greater number, however, passed their years on Breakness, unchanging except for perhaps a slight gauntness and angularity of the bone structure. And then, inexorably the dominie would approach his Emeritus status: he would become less precise, more emotional; egocentricity would begin to triumph over the essential social accommodations; there would be outbursts of petulance, wrath, and a final megalomania—and then the Emeritus would disappear.

Beran, shy and lacking fluency, at first held

aloof from the discussions. As he acquired facility with the language, he began to join the discussions, and after a period of polemic trouncings, found himself capable of fair success. These experiences provided him the first glow of pleasure he had known on Breakness.

Interrelationships between the students were formal, neither amiable nor contentious. Of intense interest to the youth of Breakness was the subject of procreation in every possible ramification. Beran, conditioned to Paonese standards of modesty, was at first distressed, but familiarity robbed the topic of its sting. He found that prestige on Breakness was a function not only of intellectual achievement but also of the number of females in one's dormitory, the number of sons which passed the acceptance tests, the degree of resemblance in physique and mind with the sire, and the sons' own achievements. Certain of the dominies were highly respected in these regards, and ever more regularly was the name of Lord Palafox heard.

When Beran entered his fifteenth year, Palafox's repute rivaled that of Lord Karollen Vampellte, High Dominie of the Institute. Beran was unable to restrain a sense of identification and so pride.

A year or two after puberty, a youth of the Institute might expect to be presented with a girl by his sire. Beran, attaining this particu-

lar stage in his development, was a youth of
pleasant appearance, rather slender, almost
frail. His hair was a dark brown, his eyes gray
and wide, his expression pensive. Due to his
exotic origin and a certain native diffidence,
he was seldom party to what small group
activity existed. When he finally felt the pre-
adult stirrings in his blood and began to think
of the girl whom he might expect to receive
from Palafox, he went alone to the space
terminal.

He chose a day on which the transport from
Journal was due, and arriving just as the lighter dropped down from the orbiting ship, found
the terminal in apparent confusion. To one
side, in quiet, almost stolid ranks stood women
at the end of their indentures, together with
their girl children and those boys who had
failed the Breakness tests. Their ages ranged
from twenty-five to thirty-five; they would now
return to their home-worlds as wealthy women,
with most of their lives before them.

The lighter slid its nose under the shelter,
and the doors opened; young women trooped
forth, looking curiously to right and left, swaying and dancing to the blast of the wind. Un-
like the women at the ends of their indentures, these were volatile and nervous, parad-
ing their defiance, concealing their apprehension. Their eyes roved everywhere, curious to
find what sort of man would claim them.

Beran looked on in fascination.

A squad-leader gave a terse order; the incoming broods filed across the terminal to be registered and receipted; Beran strolled closer, sidling toward one of the younger girls. She turned wide sea-green eyes on him, then swung suddenly away. Beran moved forward—then stopped short. These women puzzled him. There was a sense of familiarity to them, the redolence of a pleasant past. He listened as they spoke among themselves. Their language was one he knew well.

He stood beside the girl. She observed him without friendliness.

"You are Paonese," Beran exclaimed in wonder. "What do Paonese women do on Breakness?"

"The same as any other."

"But this has never been the case!"

"You know very little of Pao," she said bitterly.

"No, no, I am Paonese!"

"Then you must know what occurs on Pao."

Beran shook his head. "I have been here since the death of Panarch Aiello."

She spoke in a low voice, looking off across the terminal. "You chose well, for things go poorly. Bustamonte is a madman."

"He sends women to Breakness?" Beran asked in a hushed husky voice.

"A hundred a month—we who have been dispossessed or made orphans by the turmoil."

Beran's voice failed. He tried to speak; while he was stammering a question, the woman began to move away. "Wait!" croaked Beran, running along beside. "What turmoil is this?"

"I cannot wait," the girl said bitterly. "I am indentured, I must do as I am bid."

"Where do you go? To the dormitory of what lord?"

"I am in the service of Lord Palafox."

"What is your name?" Beran demanded. "Tell me your name!"

Embarrassed and uncertain, she said nothing. Two paces more and she would be gone, lost in the anonymity of the dormitory. "Tell me your name!"

She spoke swiftly over her shoulder: "Gitan Netsko"—then passed through the door and out of his sight. The vehicle moved off the ramp, swayed in the wind, drifted down slope and was gone.

Beran walked slowly down from the terminal, a small figure on the mountainside, leaning and stumbling against the wind. He passed among the houses, and arrived at the house of Palafox.

Outside the door he hesitated, picturing the tall figure within. He summoned the whole of his resources, tapped the escutcheon plate. The door opened; he entered.

At this hour Palafox might well be in his lower study. Down the familiar steps Beran walked, past the remembered rooms of stone and valuable Breakness hardwood. At one time he had considered the house harsh and bleak; now he could see it to be subtly beautiful, perfectly suited to the environment.

As he had expected, Palafox sat in his study; and, warned by a stimulus from one of his modifications, was expecting him.

Beran came slowly forward, staring into the inquiring but unsympathetic face, and plunged immediately into the heart of his subject. It was useless to attempt deviousness with Palafox. "I was at the terminal today. I saw Paonese women, who came here unwillingly. They speak of turmoil and hardship. What is happening on Pao?"

Palafox considered Beran a moment, then nodded with faint amusement. "I see. You are old enough now to frequent the terminal. Do you find any women suitable for your personal use?"

Beran bit his lips. "I am concerned by what must be happening on Pao. Never before have our people been so degraded!"

Palafox pretended shock. "But serving a Breakness dominie is by no means degradation!"

Beran, feeling that he had scored a point on his redoubtable opponent, took heart. "Still you have not answered my question."

"That is true," said Palafox. He motioned to a chair. "Sit down—I will describe to you exactly what is taking place." Beran gingerly seated himself. Palafox surveyed him through half-closed eyes. "Your information as to turmoil and hardship on Pao is half-true. Something of this nature exists, regrettably but unavoidably."

Beran was puzzled. "There are droughts? Plagues? Famines?"

"No," said Palafox. "None of these. There is only social change. Bustamonte is embarked on a novel but courageous venture. You remember the invasion from Batmarsh?"

"Yes, but where . . ."

"Bustamonte wants to prevent any recurrence of this shameful event. He is developing a corps of warriors for the defense of Pao. For their use he has appointed the Hylanth Littoral of the continent Shraimand. The old population has been removed. A new group, trained to military ideals and speaking a new language, has taken their place. On Vidamand, Bustamonte is using similar means to create an industrial complex, in order to make Pao independent of Mercantil."

Beran fell silent, impressed by the scope of these tremendous schemes, but there were still doubts in his mind. Palafox waited patiently. Beran frowned uncertainly, bit at his knuckle, and finally blurted out: "But the Paonese have never been warriors or mechanics—they know nothing of these things! How can Bustamonte succeed with this plan?"

"You must remember," said Palafox drily, "that I advise Bustamonte."

There was an unsettling corollary to Palafox's statement—the bargain which evidently existed between himself and Bustamonte. Beran suppressed the thought of it, put it to the back of his mind. He asked in a subdued voice, "Was it necessary to drive the inhabitants from their homes?"

"Yes. There could be no tincture of the old language or the old ways."

Beran, a native Paonese, aware that mass tragedy was a commonplace of Paonese history, was able to accept the force of Palafox's explanation. "These new people—will they be true Paonese?"

Palafox seemed surprised. "Why should they not? They'll be of Paonese blood, born and bred on Pao, loyal to no other source."

Beran opened his mouth to speak, closed it again dubiously.

Palafox waited, but Beran, while patently not happy, could not find logical voice to give his emotions.

"Now tell me," said Palafox, in a different tone of voice, "how goes it at the Institute?"

"Very well, I have completed the fourth of my theses—the provost found matter to interest him in my last independent essay."

"And what was the subject?"

"An expansion upon the Paonese vitality-word *praesens*, with an effort at transposition into Breakness attitudes."

Palafox's voice took on something of an edge. "And how do you so easily analyze the mind of Breakness?"

Beran, surprised at the implied disapproval, nevertheless answered without diffidence. "Surely it is a person such as I, neither of Pao nor of Breakness, but part of both, who can make comparisons."

"Better, in this case, than one such as I?"

Beran considered carefully. "I have no basis for comparison."

Palafox stared hard at him, then laughed. "I must call for your essay and study it. Are you determined yet upon the basic direction of your studies?"

Beran shook his head. "There are a dozen possibilities. At the moment I find myself absorbed by human history, by the possibility of pattern and its peculiar absence. But I have much to learn, many authorities to consult, and perhaps this form will eventually make itself known to me."

"It seems that you follow the inspiration of Dominie Arbursson, the Teleologist."

"I have studied his ideas," said Beran.

"Ah, and they do not interest you?"

Beran made another careful reply. "Lord

Arbursson is a Breakness dominie. I am Paonese."

Palafox laughed shortly. "The form of your statement implies an equivalence between the two conditions of being."

Beran, wondering at Palafox's testiness, made no comment.

"Well then," said Palafox, a trifle heavily, "it seems as if you are going your way and making progress." He eyed Beran up and down. "And you have been frequenting the terminal."

Beran, influenced by Paonese attitudes, blushed. "Yes."

"Then it becomes time that you began practicing procreation. No doubt you are well-versed in the necessary theory?"

"The students of my age talk of little else," said Beran. "If it please you, Lord Palafox, today at the terminal . . ."

"So now we learn the source of your trouble, eh? Well then, what is her name?"

"Gitan Netsko," Beran said huskily.

"Await me here." Palafox strode from the room.

Twenty minutes later he appeared in the doorway, signaled to Beran. "Come."

A domed air-car waited outside the house. Within, a small forlorn figure sat huddled. Palafox fixed Beran with a stern gaze.

"It is customary that sire provide son with education, his first female, and a modicum of dispassionate counsel. You already are profiting by the education—in the car is the one of your choice, and you may also retain the car. Here is the counsel, and mark it well, for never will you receive more valuable! Monitor your thoughts for traces of Paonese mysticism and sentimentality. Isolate these impulses—make yourself aware of them, but do not necessarily try to expunge them, because then their influence subverts to a deeper, more basic, level." Palafox held up his hand in one of the striking Breakness gestures. "I have now acquitted myself of my responsibilities. I wish you a successful career, a hundred sons of great achievement, and the respectful envy of your peers." Palafox bowed his head formally.

"Thank you," said Beran with equal formality. He turned and walked through the howl of the wind to the car.

The girl, Gitan Netsko, looked up as he entered, then turned her eyes away and stared out across the great Wind River.

Beran sat quiet, his heart too full for words. At last he reached out, took her hand. It was limp and cool; her face was quiet.

Beran tried to convey what was in his mind. "You are now in my care. . . . I am Paonese. . . ."

"Lord Palafox has assigned me to serve you," she said in a measured passionless voice.

Beran sighed. He felt miserable and full of qualms: the Paonese mysticism and sentimentality Palafox had expressly counseled him to suppress. He raised the car into the wind; then slid downhill to the dormitory. He conducted her to his room with conflicting emotions.

They stood in the austere little room, surveying each other uneasily. "Tomorrow," said Beran, "I will arrange for better quarters. It is too late today."

The girl's eyes had been growing fuller and fuller; now she sank upon the couch, and suddenly began to weep—slow tears of loneliness, humiliation, grief.

Beran, feeling full of guilt, went to sit beside her. He took her hand, stroked it, muttered consoling words, which she clearly never heard. It was his first intimate contact with grief; it disturbed him tremendously.

The girl was speaking in a low monotone. "My father was a kind man—never did he harm a living creature. Our home was almost a thousand years old. Its timber was black with age and all the stone grew moss. We lived beside Mervan Pond, with our yarrow field behind, and our plum orchard up the slope of Blue Mountain. When the agents came and ordered us to leave, my father was astonished. Leave our old home? A joke! Never! They spoke only three words and my father was angry and pale and silent. Still we did not move. And the next time they came ..." the sad voice dwindled away; tears made soft marks on Beran's arm.

"It will be mended!" said Beran.

She shook her head. "Impossible. . . . And I would as soon be dead too."

"No, never say that!" Beran sought to comfort her. He stroked her hair, kissed her cheek. He could not help himself—the contact aroused him, his caresses became more intimate. She made no resistance. Indeed she seemed to welcome the love-making as a distraction from her grief.

They awoke early in the morning dimness, while the sky was still the color of cast iron, the slope black and featureless as tar, Wind River a roaring darkness.

After awhile Beran said, "You know so very little about me—are you not curious?"

Gitan Netsko made a noncommittal sound, and Beran felt a trifle nettled.

"I am Paonese," he said earnestly. "I was born in Eiljanre fifteen years ago. Temporarily I live on Breakness."

He paused, expecting her to inquire the reason for his exile, but she turned her head, looking up through the high narrow window into the sky.

"Meanwhile I study at the Institute," said Beran. "Until last night I was uncertain—I knew not where I would specialize. Now I know! I will become a Dominie of Linguistics!"

Gitan Netsko turned her head, looked at

him. Beran was unable to read the emotion in
her eyes. They were wide eyes, sea-green, striking in her pale face. He knew her to be younger than himself by a year, but meeting her
gaze, he felt unsure, ineffectual, absurd.

"What are you thinking?" he asked plain-
tively.

She shrugged. "Very little. . . ."

"Oh, come!" He bent over her, kissed her
forehead, her cheek, her mouth. She made
neither resistance nor response. Beran began
to worry. "Do you dislike me? Have I annoyed
you?"

"No," she said in a soft voice. "How could
you? So long as I am under indenture to a
man of Breakness, my feelings mean nothing."

Beran jerked upright. "But I am no man of
Breakness! It is as I told you! I am Paonese!"

Gitan Netsko made no response and seemed
to lapse into a private world.

"Someday I will return to Pao. Perhaps soon,
who knows? You will come back with me."

She made no comment. Beran was exasper-
ated. "Don't you believe me?"

In a muffled voice she said, "If you were
truly Paonese, you would know what I believe."

Beran fell silent. At last he said, "Regard-
less of what I may be, I see you do not believe
me to be Paonese!"

She burst out furiously, "What difference
does it make? Why should you take pride in

such a claim? The Paonese are spineless mud-worms—they allow the tyrant Bustamonte to molest them, despoil them, kill them, and never do they raise a hand in protest! They take refuge like sheep in a wind, rumps to the threat. Some flee to a new continent, others . . ." she darted him a cool glance ". . . take refuge on a distant planet. I am not proud to be Paonese!"

Beran somberly rose to his feet looking blindly away from the girl. Seeing himself in his mind's-eye he grimaced: what a paltry figure he cut! There was nothing to say in his own defense; to plead ignorance and helplessness would be an ignoble bleating. Beran heaved a deep sigh, began to dress himself.

He felt a touch on his arm. "Forgive me—I know you meant no harm."

Beran shook his head, feeling a thousand years old. "I meant no harm, that is true. . . . But so is everything else you said. . . . There are so many truths—how can anyone make up his mind?"

"I know nothing of these many truths," said the girl. "I know only how I feel, and I know that if I were able I would kill Bustamonte the Tyrant!"

As early as Breakness custom allowed, Beran presented himself at the house of Palafox. One of the sons-in-residence admitted him, inquired

his business, which question Beran evaded.
There was a delay of several minutes, while
Beran waited nervously in a bleak little ante-
room near the top of the house.

Beran's instinct warned him to circumspec-
tion, to a preliminary testing of the ground—
but he knew, with a sinking feeling at the pit
of his stomach, that he lacked the necessary
finesse.

At last he was summoned and conducted
far down the escalator, into a wood-paneled
morning room, where Palafox, in a somber
blue robe, sat eating bits of hot pickled fruit.
He regarded Beran without change of expression, nodded almost imperceptibly. Beran
made the customary gesture of respect and
spoke in the most serious voice he could mus-
ter: "Lord Palafox, I have come to an important decision."

Palafox looked at him blankly. "Why should
you not? You have reached the age of responsibility, and none of your decisions should be
frivolous."

Beran said doggedly, "I want to return to
Pao."

Palafox made no immediate response, but it
was clear that Beran's request struck no sympathetic fire. Then he said in his driest voice,
"I am astonished at your lack of wisdom."

Again the subtle diversion, the channeling
of opposing energy into complicated paths.

But the device was wasted on Beran. He plowed ahead. "I have been thinking about Bustamonte's program, and I am worried. It may bring benefits—but I feel there is something abnormal and unnatural at work."

Palafox's mouth compressed. "Assuming the correctness of your sensations—what could you do to counter this tendency?"

"I am the true Panarch, am I not? Is not Bustamonte merely Ayudor-Senior? If I appear before him, he must obey me."

"In theory. How will you assert your identity? Suppose he claims you to be a madman, an imposter?"

Beran stood silently; it was a point which he had not considered.

Palafox continued relentlessly. "You would be subaqueated, your life would be quenched. What would you have achieved?"

"Perhaps I would not announce myself to Bustamonte. If I came down on one of the islands—Ferai or Viamne . . ."

"Very well. Suppose you convinced a certain number of persons of your identity, Bustamonte would still resist. You might precipitate civil war. If you consider Bustamonte's action ruthless, consider your own intentions in this light."

Beran smiled. "You do not understand the Paonese. There would be no war. Bustamonte would merely find himself without authority."

Palafox did not relish the correction of

Beran's views. "And if Bustamonte learns of your coming, and meets the ship with a squad of neutraloids, what then?"

"How would he know?"

Palafox ate a bit of spiced apple. He spoke deliberately. "I would tell him."

"Then you oppose me?"

Palafox smiled his faint smile. "Not unless you act against my interests—which at this time coincide with those of Bustamonte."

"What are your interests, then?" cried Beran. "What do you hope to achieve?"

"On Breakness," said Palafox softly, "those are questions which one never asks."

Beran was silent for a moment. Then he turned away, exclaiming bitterly, "Why did you bring me here? Why did you sponsor me at the Institute?"

Palafox, the basic conflict now defined, relaxed and sat at his ease. "Where is the mystery? The able strategist provides himself as many tools and procedures as possible. Your function was to serve as a lever against Bustamonte, if the need should arise."

"And now I am of no further use to you?"

Palafox shrugged. "I am no seer—I cannot read the future. But my plans for Pao . . ."

"*Your* plans for Pao!" Beran interjected.

". . . develop smoothly. My best estimate is that you are no longer an asset, for now you threaten to impede the smooth flow of events.

It is best, therefore, that our basic relationship is clear. I am by no means your enemy,
but neither do our interests coincide. You have
no cause for complaint. Without my help you
would be dead. I have provided you suste-
nance, shelter, an unexcelled education. I will
continue to sponsor your career unless you
take action against me. There is no more to
say."

Beran rose to his feet, bowed in formal respect. He turned to depart, hesitated, looked
back. Meeting the black eyes, wide and burning, he felt shock. This was not the notably
rational Dominie Palafox, intelligent, highly-
modified, second in prestige only to Lord Dominie Vampellte; this man was strange and
wild, and radiated a mental force over and
beyond the logic of normality.

Beran returned to his cubicle, where he
found Gitan Netsko sitting on the stone win-
dow-ledge, chin on knees, arms clasped around
her ankles.

She looked up as he came in, and in spite of
his depression, Beran felt a pleasurable, if wist-
ful, thrill of ownership. She was charming, he
thought: a typical Paonese of the Vinelands,
slender and clear-skinned with fine bones and
precisely-modeled features. Her expression was
unreadable; he had no hint as to how she
regarded him, but this was how it went on

Pao, where the intimate relationships of youth were traditionally shrouded in indirection and ambiguity. A lift of an eyebrow could indicate raging passion; a hesitancy, a lowered pitch of the voice absolute aversion. . . . Abruptly Beran said, "Palafox will not permit my return to Pao."

"No? And so then?"

He walked to the window, looked somberly across the mist-streaming chasm. "So then—I will depart without his permission. . . . As soon as opportunity offers."

She surveyed him skeptically. "And if you return—what is the use of that?"

Beran shook his head dubiously. "I don't know exactly. I would hope to restore order, bring about a return to the old ways."

She laughed sadly, without scorn. "It is a fine ambition. I hope I shall see it."

"I hope you shall, too."

"But I am puzzled. How will you effect all this?"

"I don't know. In the simplest case I will merely issue the orders." Observing her expression, Beran exclaimed. "You must understand, I am the true Panarch. My uncle Bustamonte is an assassin—he killed my father, Aiello."

XI

BERAN'S RESOLVE to return to Pao was difficult to implement. He had neither funds to buy, nor authority to commandeer, transportation. He tried to beg passage for himself and the girl; he was rebuffed and ridiculed. At last frustrated, he sulked in his rooms, ignoring his studies, exchanging hardly a word with Gitan Netsko, who spent most of her time staring blankly along the windy chasm.

Three months passed. And one morning Gitan Netsko remarked that she thought herself pregnant.

Beran took her to the clinic, registered her for the prenatal regimen. His appearance aroused surprise and amusement among the staff of the clinic. "You bred the child without assistance? Come now, tell us: who is the actual father?"

"She is indentured to me," Beran stated, indignant and angry. "I am the father!"

"Forgive our skepticism, but you appear hardly the age."

"The facts seem to contradict you," Beran retorted.

"We shall see, we shall see." They motioned to Gitan Netsko. "Into the laboratory with you."

At the last moment the girl became afraid. "Please, I'd rather not."

"It's all part of our usual routine," the reception clerk assured her. "Come, this way, if you please."

"No, no," she muttered, and shrank back. "I don't want to go!"

Beran was puzzled. He turned to the reception clerk. "Is it necessary that she go now?"

"Certainly!" said the clerk in exasperation. "We make standard tests against possible genetic discord or abnormality. These factors, if discovered now, prevent difficulty later."

"Can't you wait until she is more composed?"

"We'll give you a sedative." They laid hands on the girl's shoulder. As they took her away, she turned an anguished glance back to Beran that told him many things that she had never spoken.

Beran waited—an hour, two hours. He went to the door, knocked. A young medic came forth and Beran thought to detect discomfort in his expression.

"Why the delay? Surely by now . . ."

The medic held up his hand. "I fear that there have been complications. It appears that you have not sired after all."

A chill began to spread through Beran's viscera. "What sort of complications?"

The medic moved away, back through the door. "You had best return to your dormitory. There is no need to wait longer."

Gitan Netsko was taken to the laboratory, where she submitted to a number of routine tests. Presently she was laid, back down, on a pallet and rolled underneath a heavy machine. An electric field damped her cephalic currents, anaesthetized her while the machine dipped an infinitesimally thin needle into her abdomen, searched into the embryo and withdrew a half-dozen cells.

The field died; Gitan Netsko returned to consciousness. She was now conveyed to a waiting room, while the genetic structure of the embryonic cells were evaluated, categorized and classified by a calculator.

The signal returned: "A male child, normal in every phase. Class AA expectancy." The index to her own genetic type was shown, and likewise, that of the father.

The operator observed the paternal index without particular interest, then looked again. He called an associate, they chuckled, and one of them spoke into a communicator.

The voice of Lord Palafox returned. "A Paonese girl? Show me her face. . . . I remember—I bred her before I turned her over to my ward. It is definitely my child?"

"Indeed, Lord Palafox. There are few indices we are more familiar with."

"Very well—I will convey her to my dormitory."

Palafox appeared ten minutes later. He bowed with formal respect to Gitan Netsko, who surveyed him with fear.

Palafox spoke politely. "It appears that you are carrying my child, of Class AA expectancy, which is excellent. I will take you to my personal laying-in ward, where you will get the best of care."

She looked at him blankly. "It is your child that I carry?"

"So the analyzers show. If you bear well, you will earn a bonus. I assure you, you will never find me niggardly."

She jumped to her feet, eyes blazing. "This is horror—I won't bear such a monster!"

She ran wildly down the room, out the door, with the medic and Palafox coming behind.

She sped past the door which led to the room where Beran waited, but saw only the great spine of the escalator which communicated with levels above and below.

At the landing she paused, looked behind with a wild grimace. The spare shape of Palafox was only a few yards behind. "Halt!" he cried in passion. "You carry my child!"

She made no answer, but turning, looked down the staircase. She closed her eyes, sighed, let herself fall forward. Down and down she rolled, pumping and thudding, while Palafox stared after her in amazement. At last she came to rest, far below, a limp huddle, oozing blood.

The medics took her up on a litter, but the child was gone and Palafox departed in disgust.

There were other injuries, and since Gitan Netsko had decided on death, the Breakness medicine could not force life upon her. . . .

When Beran returned the next day he was told that the child had been that of Lord Palafox; that, upon learning of this fact, the girl had returned to the dormitory of Palafox in order to collect the birth-bonus. The actual circumstances were rigidly suppressed; in the society of Breakness Institute, nothing could so reduce a man's prestige, or make him more ridiculous in the eyes of his peers, than an episode of this sort: that a woman had killed herself rather than bear his child.

For a week Beran sat in his cubicle, or wandered the windy streets as long as his flesh could withstand the chill. And indeed it was by no conscious will that his feet took him trudging back the dormitory.

Never had life seemed so dismal a panorama. He reacted from his stupor and dullness with an almost vicious emotion. He flung himself into his work at the Institute, wadding knowledge into his mind to serve as poultice against his grief.

Two years passed. Beran grew taller; the bones of his face showed hard through his skin. Gitan Netsko receded in his memory, to become a bitter-sweet dream.

One or two odd things occurred during these years—affairs for which he could find no explanation. Once he met Palafox in a corridor of the Institute; Palafox turned him a glance so chill that Beran stared in wonder. It was himself who bore the grievance, not Palafox. Why then, Palafox's animosity?

On another occasion he looked up from a desk in the library to find a group of high-placed dominies standing at the side, looking at him. They were amused and intent, as if they shared a private joke. Indeed this was the case—and poor Gitan Netsko had provided its gist. The facts of her passing had been too good to keep, and now Beran was pointed out among the knowledgeable as the stripling who had, to paraphrase, "out-bred" Lord Palafox to such an extent that a girl had killed herself rather than return to Palafox.

The joke at last became stale and half-forgotten; only emotional scar-tissue remained.

After the passing of Gitan Netsko, Beran once more began to frequent the space-port—as much in hopes of garnering news of Pao as watching the incoming women. On his fourth visit he was startled to see debarking from the lighter a large group of young men—forty or fifty—almost certainly Paonese. When he drew close enough to hear their speech, his assumption was verified; they were Paonese indeed!

He approached one of the group as they stood waiting for registration, a tall sober-faced youth no older than himself. He forced himself to speak casually. "How goes it on Pao?"

The newcomer appraised him carefully, as if calculating how much veracity he could risk. In the end he made a non-committal reply. "As well as might be, times and conditions as they are."

Beran had expected little more. "What do you do here on Breakness, so many of you in a group?"

"We are apprentice linguists, here for advance study."

" 'Linguists'? On Pao? What innovation is this?"

The newcomer studied Beran. "You speak Paonese with a native accent. Strange you know so little of current affairs."

"I have lived on Breakness for eight years.

You are the second Paonese I have seen in this time."

"I see. . . . Well, there have been changes. Today on Pao one must know five languages merely to ask for a glass of wine."

The line advanced toward the desk. Beran kept pace, as one time before he had kept pace with Gitan Netsko. As he watched the names being noted into a register, into his mind came a notion which excited him to such an extent that he could hardly speak. . . . "How long will you study on Breakness?" he asked huskily.

"A year."

Beran stepped back, made a careful estimate of the situation. The plan seemed feasible; in any case, what could he lose? He glanced down at his clothes: typical Breakness wear. Retiring to a corner, he pulled off his blouse and singlet; by reversing their order, and allowing them to hang loose outside his trousers, he achieved an effect approximately Paonese.

He fell in at the end of the line. The youth ahead of him looked back curiously, but made no comment. Presently he came to the registration desk. The clerk was a young Institute don four or five years older than himself. He seemed bored with his task and barely glanced up when Beran came to the desk.

"Name?" asked the clerk in heavy Paonese.

"Ercole Paraio."

The clerk broodingly scanned the list. "What are the symbols?"

Beran spelled forth the fictitious name.

"Strange," muttered the clerk. "It's not on the roster.... Some inefficient fool...." His voice dwindled; he twitched the sheet. "The symbols again?"

Beran spelled the name, and the clerk added it to the registration manifest. "Very well— here is your pass-book. Carry it at all times on Breakness. You will surrender it when you return to Pao."

Beran followed the others to a waiting vehicle, and in the new identity of Ercole Paraio, rode down the slope to a new dormitory. It seemed a fantastic hope.... And yet—why not? The apprentice-linguists had no reason to accuse him; their minds were occupied by the novelty of Breakness. Who would investigate Beran, the neglected ward of Palafox? No one. Each student of the Institute was responsible only to himself. As Ercole Paraio, he could find enough freedom to maintain the identity of Beran Panasper, until such time that Beran should disappear.

Beran, with the other apprentice linguists from Pao, was assigned a sleeping cubicle and a place at the refectory table.

The class was convocated the next morning in a bare stone hall roofed with clear glass.

The wan sunlight slanted in, cut the wall with a division between light and shade.

A young Institute don named Finisterle, one of Palafox's many sons, appeared to address the group. Beran had noticed him many times— tall, even more gaunt than the Breakness norm, with Palafox's prow-like nose and command- ing forehead, but with brooding brown eyes and a dark-oak skin inherited from his name- less mother. He spoke in a quiet, almost gen- tle voice, looking from face to face, and Beran wondered whether Finisterle would recognize him.

"In a sense, you are an experimental group," said Finisterle. "It is necessary that many Paonese learn many languages swiftly. Train- ing here on Breakness may be a means to this end.

"Perhaps in some of your minds is confu- sion. Why, you ask, must we learn three new languages?

"In your case, the answer is simple: you will be an elite managerial corps—you will coordinate, you will expedite, you will instruct.

"But this does not completely answer your question. Why, you ask, must anyone learn a new language? The response to this question is found in the science of dynamic linguistics. Here are the basic precepts, which I will enun- ciate without proof or argument, and which, for the time being at least, you must accept arbitrarily.

"Language determines the pattern of thought, the sequence in which various types of reactions follow acts.

"No language is neutral. All languages contribute impulse to the mass mind, some more vigorously than others. I repeat, we know of no 'neutral' language—and there is no 'best' or 'optimum' language, although Language A may be more suitable for Context X than Language B.

"In an even wider frame of reference, we note that every language imposes a certain world-view upon the mind. What is the 'true' world-picture? Is there a language to express this 'true' word-picture? First, there is no reason to believe that a 'true' world-picture, if it existed, would be a valuable or advantageous tool. Second, there is no standard to define the 'true' world-picture. 'Truth' is contained in the preconceptions of him who seeks to define it. Any organization of ideas whatever presupposes a judgment on the world."

Beran sat listening in vague wonder. Finisterle spoke in Paonese, with very little of the staccato Breakness accent. His ideas were considerably more moderate and equivocal than any others that Beran had heard expressed around the Institute.

Finisterle spoke further, describing the routine of study, and as he spoke it seemed that his eyes rested ever more frequently and frowningly upon Beran. Beran's heart began to sink.

But when Finisterle had finished his speech, he made no move to accost Beran, and seemed, rather, to ignore him. Beran thought perhaps he had gone unrecognized after all.

Beran tried to maintain at least the semblance of his former life at the Institute, and made himself conspicuous about the various studios, research libraries and classrooms, so that there should be no apparent diminution in his activity.

On the third day, entering a depiction booth at the library, he almost bumped into Finisterle emerging. The two looked eye to eye. Then Finisterle stepped aside with a polite excuse, and went his way. Beran, his face hot as fire, entered the booth, but was too upset to code for the film he had come to study.

Then the next morning, as luck would have it, he was assigned to a recitation class conducted by Finisterle, and found himself seated across a dark teak table from this ubiquitous son of Palafox.

Finisterle's expression did not change; he was grave and polite when he spoke to Beran— but Beran thought he saw a sardonic spark in the other man's eyes. Finisterle seemed too grave, too solicitous, too courteous.

Beran's nerves could stand no further suspense. After the class he waited in his seat while the others departed.

Finisterle, likewise, had risen to leave. He lifted his eyebrows in polite surprise when Beran spoke to him. "You have a question, Student Paraio?"

"I want to know what you plan toward me. Why don't you report me to Palafox?"

Finisterle made no pretense of incomprehension. "The fact that as Beran Panasper you attend the Institute, and as Ercole Paraio you study languages with the Paonese? What should I plan, why should I report you?"

"I don't know. I wonder if you will."

"I cannot understand how your conduct affects me."

"You must know I am here as ward of Lord Palafox."

"Oh indeed. But I have no mandate to guard his interests. Even," he added delicately, "if I desired to do so."

Beran looked his surprise. Finisterle went on in a soft voice. "You are Paonese; you do not understand us of Breakness. We are total individuals—each has his private goal. The Paonese word 'cooperation' has no counterpart on Breakness. How would I advance myself by monitoring your case to Sire Palafox? Such an act is irreversible. I commit myself without perceptible advantage. If I say nothing, I have alternate channels always open."

Beran stammered. "Do I understand then, that you do not intend to report me?"

Finisterle nodded. "Not unless it reacts to my advantage. And this I can not envision at the moment."

XII

A YEAR PASSED—a year of anxiety, inward triumph, carefully stifled hope; a year of artifice, of intense study in which the necessity to learn seemed to kindle the powers of learning; a year during which Beran Panasper, the Paonese exile, was an attentive if irregular student at the Institute and Ercole Paraio, the Paonese apprentice linguist, made swift progress in three new languages: Valiant, Technicant and Cogitant.

To Beran's surprise and to his great advantage, Cogitant proved to be the language of Breakness, modified considerably against the solipsism latent in the original tongue.

Beran thought it best not to display ignorance of current conditions on Pao, and restrained his questions. Nevertheless, by circuitous methods, he learned much of what was transpiring on Pao.

On sections of two continents, the Hylanth Littoral of Shraimand, and along the shores of Zelambre Bay on the north coast of Vidamand, dispossession, violence and the misery of refugee camps still continued. No one knew definitely the scope of Bustamonte's plans—no doubt as Bustamonte intended. In both areas, the original population had been and were being disestablished, while the enclave of new speech expanded, a tide pressing against the retreating shores of the old Paonese customs. The areas affected were still comparatively small, and the new populations very young: children in the first and second octads of life, guided by a spare cadre of linguists who under pain of death spoke only the new language.

In subdued voices the apprentices recalled scenes of anguish: the absolute passive obduracy of the population, even in the face of starvation; the reprisals, effected with true Paonese disregard for the individual life.

In other respects Bustamonte had proved himself a capable ruler. Prices were stable, the civil service was reasonably efficient. His personal scale of living was splendid enough to gratify the Paonese love of pomp, but not so extravagantly magnificent as to bankrupt the treasury. Only on Shraimand and Vidamand was there real dissatisfaction—and here of course dissatisfaction was a mild word for the sullen rancor, the pain and grief.

Of the infant societies which in due course would expand across the vacated lands, little was known and Beran found it hard to distinguish between speculation and fact.

A person born to the Paonese tradition inherited insensitivity toward human suffering—not so much callousness as an intuition of fate. Pao was a world of vast numbers and cataclysm automatically affected great masses of people. A Paonese hence might be touched by the plight of a bird with a broken wing, even as he ignored news of ten thousand drowning in a tidal wave.

Beran's Paonese endowment had been modified by his education; for no one could regard the population of Breakness as anything other than a set of discrete units. Perhaps for this reason he was moved by the woe of Shraimand and Vidamand. Hate, an element hitherto foreign to his nature, began to find a place in his mind. Bustamonte, Palafox—these men had vast horrors to answer for!

The year moved to its completion. Beran, through a combination of natural intelligence, zeal and his prior knowledge of the Breakness language, achieved a creditable record as apprentice linguist, and likewise sustained something of his previous program. In effect Beran lived two distinct existences, each insulated from the other. His old life, as student at Breakness Institute, offered no problem, since no one spent an iota of attention on any but his own problems.

As an apprentice linguist, the situation was more difficult. His fellow students were Paonese, gregarious and inquisitive, and Beran won a reputation for eccentricity, for he had neither time nor inclination to join the spare time recreations.

In a jocular moment the students contrived a bastard mish-mash of a language, assembled from scraps of Paonese, Cogitant, Valiant, Technicant, Mercantil and Batch, with a syncretic syntax and heterogenous vocabulary. The patchwork tongue was known as Pastiche.

The students vied in fluency and used it to the disapproval of the instructors, who felt that the effort might better be spent in their studies. The students, referring to the Valiants, the Technicants and the Cogitants, argued that in all logic and consistency the Interpreters should likewise speak a characteristic tongue—so why not Pastiche?

The instructors agreed in principle, but objected to Pastiche as a formless mélange, a hodge-podge without style or dignity. The students were unconcerned, but nevertheless made amused attempts to contrive style and dignity for their creation.

Beran mastered Pastiche with the others, but took no part in its formation. With other demands on his attention, he had small energy for linguistic recreations. And ever as the time of return to Pao drew near, Beran's nerves tautened.

One month remained, then a week, and the linguists spoke of nothing but Pao. Beran remained apart from the others, pale and anxious, gnawing his lips.

He met Finisterle in one of the dark corridors, and stopped short. Would Finisterle, now reminded, report him; would Finisterle set at nought his work of an entire year? But Finisterle walked past, gaze fixed on some inner image.

Four days, three days, two days—and then during the final recitations the instructor exploded a bombshell. The shock came with such sudden devastation that Beran was frozen in his seat and a pink fog blurred his vision.

". . . you will now hear the eminent dominie who initiated the program. He will explain the scope of your work, the responsibilities that are yours. Here is Lord Palafox."

Palafox strode into the room, looking neither right nor left. Beran crouched helplessly in his seat, a rabbit hoping to evade the notice of an eagle.

Palafox bowed formally to the class, making a casual survey of faces. Beran sat with head ducked behind the youth ahead; Palafox's eyes did not linger in his direction.

"I have followed your progress," said Palafox. "You have done creditably. Your presence here on Breakness was frankly an experiment, and your achievements have been compared to the work of similar groups studying on Pao. Apparently the Breakness atmosphere is a stimulus—your work has been appreciably superior. I understand that you have even evolved a characteristic language of your own—Pastiche." He smiled indulgently. "It is an ingenious idea, and though the tongue lacks elegance, a real achievement.

"I assume that you understand the magnitude of your responsibilities. You comprise nothing less than the bearings on which the machinery of Pao will run. Without your services, the new social mechanisms of Pao could not mesh, could not function."

He paused, surveyed his audience; again Beran ducked his head.

Palafox continued in a slightly different tone of voice. "I have heard many theories to explain Panarch Bustamonte's innovations, and they have been for the most part fallacious. The actuality is basically simple, yet grand in scope. In the past, Paonese society was a uniform organism with weaknesses that inevitably attracted predators. The new diversity creates strength in every direction, protects the areas of former weakness. Such is our design—but how well we succeed only the future can tell. You linguists will contribute greatly to any eventual success. You must school yourselves to flexibility. You must understand the peculiarities of each of the new Paonese societies, for your main task will be to reconcile conflicting interpretations of the same phenomena. In a large measure your efforts will determine the future of Pao."

He bowed once more and marched for the door. Beran watched him approach with thumping heart. He passed an arm's length away; Beran could feel the air of his passage. With the utmost difficulty, he prevented himself from hiding his face in his hands. Palafox's head did not turn; he left the room without slackening his stride.

On the day following, the class with great jubilation departed the dormitory and rode the air-bus to the terminal. Among them, concealed by his identity with the others, was Beran.

The class entered the terminal, filed toward the checkoff desk. The line moved forward; his mates spoke their names, turned in their pass-books, received passage vouchers, departed through the gate into the waiting lighter. Beran came to the desk. "Ercole Paraio," he said huskily, putting his pass-book down.

"Ercole Paraio." The clerk checked off the name, pushed across a voucher.

Beran took the voucher with trembling fingers, moved forward, walked as fast as he dared to the gate. He looked neither right nor left, afraid to meet the sardonic gaze of Lord Palafox.

He passed through the gate, into the lighter. Presently the port closed, the lighter rose from the rock-melt flat, swung to the blast of the wind. Up and away from Breakness, up to the orbiting ship. And finally Beran dared hope that his plan of a year's duration, his scheme to escape Breakness, might succeed.

The linguists transferred into the ship, the lighter fell away. A pulse, a thud—the voyage had begun.

XIII

THE SMALL WHITE sun dwindled, became a single glitter in the myriad; the ship floated in black space, imperceptibly shifting through the stars of the cluster.

At last yellow Auriol grew bright, tended by blue-green Pao. Beran could not leave the bullseye. He watched the world expand, lurch from a disk to a sphere. He traced the configuration of the eight continents, put names to a hundred islands, located the great cities. Nine years had passed—almost half of his life; he could not hope to find Pao the world of his recollections.

What if his absence from Breakness Institute had been detected, what if Palafox had communicated with Bustamonte? It was an apprehension that Beran had toyed with all during the voyage. If it were accurate, then awaiting the ship would be a squad of Mama-

rone, and Beran's homecoming would be a
glimpse or two of the countryside, a lift, a
thrust, the rushing air with cloud and sky
whirling above, the wet impact, the deepen-
ing blue of ocean water as he sank to his
death.

The idea seemed not only logical but likely.
The lighter drew alongside; Beran went aboard.
The other linguists broke into an old Paonese
chant, waggishly rendered into Pastiche.

The lighter eased down upon the field; the
exit ports opened. The others tumbled hap-
pily forth; Beran pulled himself to his feet,
warily followed. There was no one at hand
but the usual attendants. He drew a great
breath, looked all around the field. The time
was early afternoon; fleecy clouds floated in a
sky which was the very essence of blue. The
sun fell warm on his face. Beran felt an almost religious happiness. He would never leave
Pao again, in life or in death; if subaqueation
awaited him, he preferred it to life on Breakness.

The linguists marched off the field, into the
shabby old terminal. There was no one to
meet them, a fact which only Beran, accustomed to the automatic efficiency of Breakness,
found extraordinary. Looking around the faces
of his fellows, he thought, I am changed.
Palafox did his worst upon me. I love Pao, but
I am no longer Paonese. I am tainted with the

flavor of Breakness; I can never be truly and wholly a part of this world again—or of any other world. I am dispossessed, eclectic; I am Pastiche.

Beran separated himself from the others, went to the portal, looked down the tree-shaded boulevard toward Eiljanre. He could step forth, lose himself in a moment.

But where would he go? If he appeared at the palace, he would receive the shortest of shrift. Beran had no wish to farm, to fish, to carry loads. Thoughtfully he turned back, rejoined the linguists.

The official welcoming committee arrived; one of the dignitaries performed a congratulatory declamation, and the linguists made formal appreciation. They were then ushered aboard a bus and taken to one of the rambling Eiljanre inns.

Beran, scanning the streets, was puzzled; he saw only the usual Paonese ease. Naturally, this was Eiljanre, not the resettled areas of Shraimand and Vidamand—but surely the sheer reflection of Bustamonte's tyranny must leave a mark! Yet . . . the faces along the avenue were placid.

The bus entered the Cantatrino, a great park with three artificial mountains and a lake, the memorial of an ancient Panarch for his dead daughter, the fabulous Can. The bus passed a moss-draped arch, where the park authority

had arranged a floral portrait of Panarch Bustamonte. Someone had expressed his feelings
with a handful of black slime. A small sign—
but it revealed much, for the Paonese seldom
made political judgments.

Ercole Paraio was assigned to the Progress
School at Cloeopter, on the shores of Zelambre
Bay, at the north of Vidamand. This was the
area designated by Bustamonte to be the manufacturing and industrial center for all Pao.
The school was located in an ancient stone
monastery, built by the first settlers to a purpose long forgotten.

In the great cool halls, full of green leaf-
filtered sunlight, children of all ages lived to
the sound of the Technicant language, and
were instructed according to a special doctrine of casuality in the use of power machinery, mathematics, elementary science,
engineering and manufacturing processes. The
classes were conducted in well-equipped rooms
and work-shops; although the students were
quartered in hastily erected dormitories of
poles and canvas to either slde of the monastery. Girls and boys alike wore maroon cover-
alls and cloth caps, studied and worked with
adult intensity. After hours there were no re-
straints upon their activities so long as they
remained on school grounds.

The students were fed, clothed, housed and

furnished only with the essentials. If they desired luxuries, play equipment, special tools, private rooms, these could be earned by producing articles for use elsewhere in Pao, and almost all of the students' spare time was devoted to small industrial ventures. They produced toys, pottery, simple electrical devices, aluminum ingots reduced from nearby ore, and even periodicals printed in Technicant. A group of eight-year students had joined in a more elaborate project, a plant to extract minerals from the ocean, and to this end spent all their funds for the necessary equipment.

The instructors were for the most part young Breakness dons. From the first, Beran was perplexed by a quality he was unable to locate, let alone identify; only after he had lived at Cloeopter two months did the source of the oddness come to him. It lay in the similarity which linked these Breakness dons. Once Beran had come this far, total enlightenment followed. These youths were all sons of Palafox. By all tradition they should be engrossed in their most intensive studies at the Institute, preparing themselves for the Authority, earning modifications. Beran found the entire situation mysterious.

His own duties were simple enough, and in terms of Paonese culture, highly rewarding. The director of the school, an appointee of Bustamonte's, in theory, controlled the scope and policy of the school, but his responsibility was only nominal. Beran served as his interpreter, translating into Technicant such remarks that the director saw fit to make. For this service he was housed in a handsome cottage of cobbles and hand-hewn timber, a former farmhouse, paid a good salary and allowed a special uniform of gray-green with black and white trim.

A year passed. Beran took a melancholy interest in his work, and even found himself participating in the ambitions and plans of the students. He tried to compensate by describing with cautious enthusiasm the ideals of old Pao, but met blank unconcern. More interesting were the technical miracles they believed he must have witnessed in the Breakness laboratories.

During one of his holidays Beran made a dolorous pilgrimage to the old home of Gitan Netsko, a few miles inland. With some difficulty he found the old farm beside Mervan Pond. It was now deserted; the timber dry, the fields of yarrow overgrown with thief-grass. He seated himself on a rotting bench under a low tree, and to his mind came sad images. . . .

He climbed the slope of Blue Mountain, looked back over the valley. The solitude astonished him. Across all the horizon, over a fertile land once thronged with population, there was now no movement other than the flight of birds. Millions of human beings had been removed, most to other continents, but others had preferred to lie with their ancestral earth over them. And the flower of the land—the most beautiful and intelligent of the girls—had been transported to Breakness, to pay the debts of Bustamonte.

Beran despondently returned to Zelambre Bay. Theoretically it lay within his power to rectify the injustice—if he could find some means to regain his rightful authority. The difficulties seemed insuperable. He felt inept, incapable. . . .

Driven by his dissatisfaction, he deliberately put himself in the way of danger, and journeyed north to Eiljanre. He took a room in the old Moravi Inn, on the Tidal Canal, directly opposite the walls of the Grand Palace. His hand hesitated over the register; he restrained the reckless impulse to scrawl *Beran Panasper*, and finally noted himself as Ercole Paraio.

The capital city seemed gay enough. Was it his imagination that detected an underlying echo of anger, uncertainty, hysteria? Perhaps not: the Paonese lived in the present, as the syntax of their language and the changeless rhythm of the Paonese day impelled them.

In a mood of cynical curiosity, he checked through the archives of the Muniment Library. Nine years back, he found the last mention of his name: "During the night the alien assassins poisoned the beloved young Medallion. Thus, tragically, the direct succession of the Panaspers ends, and the collateral line stemming from Panarch Bustamonte begins, with all auspices indicating tenure of extreme duration."

Irresolute, unconvinced, without power to enforce any resolution or conviction he might have settled upon, Beran returned to the school on Zelambre Bay.

Another year passed by. The Technicants grew older, more numerous, and greatly more expert. Four small fabrication systems were established, producing tools, plastic sheet, industrial chemicals, meters and gauges; a dozen others were in prospect, and it seemed as if this particular phase of Bustamonte's dream, at least, were to prove successful.

At the end of two years Beran was transferred to Pon, on Nonamand, the bleak island continent in the southern hemisphere. The transfer came as an unpleasant surprise, for Beran had established an easy routine at Zelambre Bay. Even more unsettling was the discovery that routine had become preferable to change. At the age of twenty-one, was he already enervated? Where were his hopes, his resolutions; had he so easily discarded them? Angry at himself, furious at Bustamonte, he rode the

transport southeast across the rolling farm-
lands of South Vidamand, over the Plarth,
across the orchards and vines of Minamand's
Qurai Peninsula, across that long peculiar bight
known as The Serpent, over the green island
Fraevarth with its innumerable white villages,
and across the Great Sea of the South. The
Cliffs of Nonamand rose ahead, passed below,
fell behind; they flew into the barren heart of
the continent. Never before had Beran visited
Nonamand, and the wind-whipped moors cov-
ered with thunderstones, black gorse, contorted
cypress seemed completely un-Paonese.

Ahead loomed the Sgolaph Mountains, the
highest of all Pao. And suddenly they were
over ice-crusted crags of basalt, in a land of
glaciers, barren valleys, rushing white rivers.
The transport circled the shattered cusp of
Mount Droghead, swung quickly down upon a
bare plateau, and Beran had arrived at Pon.

The settlement was reminiscent in spirit, if
not in appearance, of Breakness Institute. A
number of dwellings, spread haphazardly to
the contour of the terrain, surrounding a central clot of more massive buildings. These, so
Beran learned, comprised laboratories, classrooms, a library, dormitories, refectories and
an administration building.

Almost immediately Beran conceived a vast
dislike for the settlement. Cogitant, the language spoken by the Paonese indoctrinees, was

a simplified Breakness, shorn of several quasi-conditional word-orders, and with considerably looser use of pronouns. Nonetheless the atmosphere of the settlement was pure Breakness, even to the customs affected by the "dominies"—actually high-ranking dons. The countryside, while by no means as fierce as that of Breakness, was nevertheless forbidding. A dozen times Beran contemplated requesting a transfer, but each time restrained himself. He had no wish to call attention to himself, with the possibility of exposing his true identity.

The teaching staff, like that of the Zelambre schools, consisted primarily of young Breakness dons, and, again, they were all sons of Palafox. In residence were a dozen Paonese sub-ministers, representatives of Bustamonte, and Beran's function was to maintain coordination between the two groups.

A situation which aroused considerable uneasiness in Beran was the fact that Finisterle, the Breakness don who knew Beran's true identity, also worked at Pon. Three times Beran, with pounding heart, managed to slip aside before Finisterle could notice him, but on the fourth occasion the meeting could not be avoided. Finisterle made only the most casual of acknowledgements and passed on, leaving Beran staring after him.

In the next few weeks Beran saw Finisterle

a number of times, and at last entered into guarded conversation. Finisterle's comments were the very definition of indirection.

Beran divined that Finisterle was anxious to continue his studies at the Institute, but remained at Pon for three reasons: first, it was the wish of his sire, Lord Palafox. Second, Finisterle felt that opportunity to breed sons of his own was easier on Pao than on Breakness. With so much, he was comparatively candid; the third reason was told more by his silence than his words. He seemed to regard Pao as a world in flux, a place of vast potentialities, where great power and prestige might be had by a person sufficiently deft and decisive.

What of Palafox? Beran wondered.

What of Palafox indeed, Finisterle seemed to say, and looking off across the plateau, apparently changed the subject. "Strange to think that even these crags, the Sgolaph, will some day be eroded to peneplain. And on the other hand, the most innocent hillock may erupt into a volcano."

These concepts were beyond dispute, said Beran.

Finisterle propounded another apparently paradoxical law of nature: "The more forceful and capacious the brain of a dominie, the more wild and violent its impulses when it succumbs to sclerosis and its owner becomes an Emeritus."

Several months later, Beran, leaving the administration headquarters, came face to face with Palafox.

Beran froze in his tracks; Palafox stared down from his greater height.

Summoning his composure, Beran performed the Paonese gesture of greeting. Palafox returned a sardonic acknowledgement. "I'm surprised to see you here," said Palafox. "I had assumed that you were diligently pursuing your education on Breakness."

"I learned a great deal," said Beran. "And then I lost all heart for further learning."

Palafox's eyes glinted. "Education is not achieved through the heart—it is a systematization of the mental processes."

"But I am something other than a mental process," said Beran. "I'm a man. I must reckon with the whole of myself."

Palafox was thinking, his eyes first contemplating Beran, then sliding along the line of the Sgolaph crags. When he spoke his voice was amiable. "There are no absolute certainties in this universe. A man must try to whip order into a yelping pack of probabilities, and uniform success is impossible."

Beran understood the meaning latent in Palafox's rather general remarks. "Since you had assured me that you took no further interest in my future, it was necessary that I act for myself. I did so, and returned to Pao."

Palafox nodded. "Beyond question, events took place outside the radius of my control. Still these rogue circumstances are often as advantageous as the most carefully nurtured plans."

"Please continue to neglect me in your calculations," said Beran in a carefully passionless voice. "I have learned to enjoy the sense of free action."

Palafox laughed with an untypical geniality. "Well said! And what do you think of new Pao?"

"I am puzzled. I have formed no single conviction."

"Understandable. There are a million facts at a thousand different levels to be assessed and reconciled. Confusion is inevitable unless you are driven by a basic ambition, as I am and as is Panarch Bustamonte. For us, these facts can be separated into categories: favorable and unfavorable."

He stepped back a pace, inspected Beran from head to foot. "Evidently you occupy yourself as a linguist."

Beran made a rather reluctant admission that this was so.

"If for no other reason," said Palafox, "you

should feel gratitude to me and Breakness Institute."

"Gratitude would be a misleading oversimplification."

"Possibly so," agreed Palafox. "And now, if you will excuse me, I must hurry to my appointment with the Director."

"One moment," said Beran. "I am perplexed. You seem not at all disturbed by my presence on Pao. Do you plan to inform Bustamonte?"

Palafox showed restiveness at the direct question; it was one which a Breakness dominie would never have deigned to make. "I plan no interference in your affairs." He hesitated a moment, then spoke in a new and confidential manner. "If you must know, circumstances have altered. Panarch Bustamonte becomes more headstrong as the years go by, and your presence may serve a useful purpose."

Beran angrily started to speak, but observing Palafox's faintly amused expression held his tongue.

"I must be on to my business," said Palafox. "Events proceed at an ever accelerating tempo. The next year or two will resolve a number of uncertainties."

Three weeks after his encounter with Palafox, Beran was transferred to Deirombona on Shraimand, where a multitude of infants, heirs to five thousand years of Paonese placidity, had been immersed in a plasm of competitiveness. Many of these were now only a few years short of manhood.

Deirombona was the oldest inhabited site on Pao, a sprawling low city of coral block in a forest of phaltorhyncus. For some reason not readily apparent, the city had been evacuated of its two million inhabitants. Deirombona Harbor remained in use; a few administrative offices had been given over to Valiant affairs; otherwise the old buildings lay stark as skeletons, bleaching under the tall trees. In the Colonial Sector, a few furtive vagrants lurked among the apartment blocks, venturing forth at night to scavenge and loot. They risked subaqueation, but since the authorities would hardly comb the maze of streets, alleys, cellars, houses, stores, warehouses, apartments and public buildings, the vagrants considered themselves secure.

The Valiant cantonments had been established at intervals up the coast, each headquarters to a legion of Myrmidons, as the Valiant warriors called themselves.

Beran had been assigned to the Deirombona Legion, and had at his disposal all the abandoned city in which to find living quarters. He selected an airy cottage on the old Lido, and was able to make himself extremely comfortable.

In many ways the Valiants were the most

interesting of all the new Paonese societies. They were easily the most dramatic. Like the Technicants of Zelambre Bay and the Cogitants of Pon, the Valiants were a race of youths, the oldest not yet Beran's age. They made a strange glittering spectacle as they strode through the Paonese sunlight, arms swinging, eyes fixed straight ahead in mystical exaltation. Their garments were intricate and of many colors, but each wore a personal device on his chest, legion insignia on his back.

During the day the young men and women trained separately, mastering their new weapons and mechanisms, but at night they ate and slept together indiscriminately, distinction being only one of rank. Emotional import was given only to organizational relationships, to competition for rank and honor.

On the evening of Beran's arrival at Deirombona, a ceremonial convocation took place at the cantonment. At the center of the parade ground a great fire burnt on a platform. Behind rose the Deirombona stele, a prism of black metal emblazoned with emblems. To either side stood ranks of young Myrmidons, and tonight all wore common garb: a plain dark gray leotard. Each carried a ceremonial lance, with a pale flickering flame in the place of a blade.

A fanfare rang out. A girl in white came forward, carrying an insignia of copper, silver and brass. While the Myrmidons knelt and bowed their heads, the girl carried the insignia three times around the fire and fixed it upon the stele.

The fire roared high. The Myrmidons rose to their feet, thrust their lances into the air. They formed into ranks and marched from the square.

The next day Beran received an explanation from his immediate superior, Sub-Strategist Gian Firanu, a soldier-of-fortune from one of the far worlds. "You witnessed a funeral—a hero's funeral. Last week Deirombona held wargames with Tarai, the next camp up the coast. A Tarai submarine had penetrated our net and was scoring against our base. All the Deirombona warriors were eager, but Lemauden was first. He dove five hundred feet with a torch and cut away the ballast. The submarine rose and was captured. But Lemauden drowned—possibly by accident."

" 'Possibly by accident'? How else? Surely the Tarai . . ."

"No, not the Tarai. But it might have been a deliberate act. These lads are wild to place their emblems on the stele—they'll do anything to create a legend."

Beran went to the window. Along the Deirombona esplanade swaggered groups of young bravos. Was this Pao? Or some fantastic world a hundred lightyears distant?

Gian Firanu was speaking; his words at first did not penetrate Beran's consciousness. "There's a new rumor going around—perhaps you've already heard it—to the effect that Bustamonte is not the true Panarch, merely Ayudor-Senior. It's said that somewhere Beran Panasper is alive and grows to manhood, gaining strength like a mythical hero. And when the hour strikes—so the supposition goes—he will come forth to fling Bustamonte into the sea."

Beran stared suspiciously, then laughed. "I had not heard this rumor. But it may well be fact, who knows?"

"Bustamonte will not enjoy the story!"

Beran laughed again, this time with genuine humor. "Better than anyone else, he'll know what truth there is in the rumor. I wonder who started this rumor."

Firanu shrugged. "Who starts any rumor? No one. They come of idle talk and misunderstanding."

"In most cases—but not all," said Beran. "Suppose this were the truth?"

"Then there is trouble ahead. And I return to Earth."

Beran heard the rumor later in the day with embellishments. The supposedly assassinated Medallion inhabited a remote island; he trained a corps of metal-clad warriors impervious to fire, steel or power; the mission of his life was to avenge his father's death—and Bustamonte walked in fear.

The talk died away, then three months later flared up again. This time the rumor told of Bustamonte's Secret police combing the planet, of thousands of young men conveyed to Eiljanre for examination, and thereafter executed, so that Bustamonte's uneasiness should not become known.

Beran had long been secure in the identity of Ercole Paraio; but now all complacency left him. He became distrait and faltered in his work. His associates observed him curiously and at last Gian Firanu inquired as to the nature of his preoccupation.

Beran muttered something about a woman in Eiljanre who was bearing his child. Firanu tartly suggested that Beran either expel so trivial a concern from his attention or take leave of absence until he felt free to concentrate on his work. Beran hastily accepted the leave of absence.

He returned to his cottage and sat several hours on the sea-flooded verandah, hoping to strike upon some sensible plan of action. The linguists might not be the first objects of suspicion, but neither would they be the last.

He could immerse himself in his role, make the identity of Ercole Paraio a trustworthy disguise. He could conceive no means to this

end, and the secret police were a good deal
more sophisticated than himself.

He could seek help from Palafox. He toyed
with the idea only an instant before discarding it with a twinge of self-disgust. He considered leaving the planet, but where would he
go—assuming that he were able to book passage?

He felt restless. There was urgency in the
air, a sense of pressure. He rose to his feet,
looked all around him: up the deserted streets,
out across the sea. He jumped down to the
beach, walked along the shore to the single
inn still functioning in Deirombona. In the
public tavern he ordered chilled wine, and
taking it out on the rattan-shaded terrace, drank
rather more deeply and hastily than was his
custom.

The air was heavy, the horizons close. From
up the street, near the building where he
worked, he saw movement, color: several men
in purple and brown.

Beran half-rose from his seat, staring. He
sank slowly back, sat limp. Thoughtfully he
sipped his wine. A dark shadow crossed his
vision. He looked up; a tall figure stood in
front of him: Palafox.

Palafox nodded a casual greeting and seated
himself. "It appears," said Palafox, "that the
history of contemporary Pao has not yet completely unfolded."

Beran said something indistinguishable. Palafox nodded his head gravely, as if Beran had put forward a profound wisdom. He indicated the three men in brown and purple who had entered the inn and were now conferring with the major-domo.

"A useful aspect of Paonese culture is the style of dress. One may determine a person's profession at a glance. Are not brown and purple the colors of the internal police?"

"Yes, that is true," said Beran. Suddenly his anxiety was gone. The worst had occurred, the tension was broken: impossible to dread what had already happened. He said in a reflective voice, "I suppose they come seeking me."

"In that case," said Palafox, "it would be wise if you departed."

"Departed? Where?"

"Where I will take you."

"No," said Beran. "I will be your tool no more."

Palafox raised his eyebrows. "What do you lose? I am offering to save your life."

"Not through concern for my welfare."

"Of course not." Palafox grinned, showing his teeth in a momentary flash. "Who but a simpleton is so guided? I serve you in order to serve myself. With this understanding I suggest we now depart the inn. I do not care to appear overtly in this affair."

"No."

Palafox was roused to anger. "What do you want?"

"I want to become Panarch."

"Yes, of course," exclaimed Palafox. "Why else do you suppose I am here? Come, let us be off, or you will be no more than carrion."

Beran rose to his feet; they departed the inn.

XIV

THE TWO MEN flew south, across the Paonese countryside, rich with ancient habitancy; then over the seas, flecked with the sails of fishing craft. League after league they flew, and neither man spoke, each contained in his own thoughts.

Beran finally broke the silence. "What is the process by which I become Panarch?"

Palafox said shortly, "The process began a month ago."

"The rumors?"

"It is necessary that the people of Pao realize that you exist."

"And why am I preferable to Bustamonte?"

Palafox laughed crisply. "In general outline, my interests would not be served by certain of Bustamonte's plans."

"And you hope that I will be more sympathetic to you?"

"You could not be more obstinate than Bustamonte."

"In what regard was Bustamonte obstinate?" Beran persisted. "He refused to concede to all your desires?"

Palafox chuckled hollowly. "Ah, you young rascal! I believe you would deprive me of all my prerogatives."

Beran was silent, reflecting that if he ever became Panarch, this indeed would be one of his primary concerns.

Palafox spoke on in a more conciliatory tone. "These affairs are for the future, and need not concern us now. At the present we are allies. To signalize this fact, I have arranged that a modification be made upon your body, as soon as we arrive at Pon."

Beran was taken by surprise. "A modification?" He considered a moment, feeling a qualm of uneasiness. "Of what nature?"

"What modification would you prefer?" Palafox asked mildly.

Beran darted a glance at the hard profile. Palafox seemed completely serious. "The total use of my brain."

"Ah," said Palafox. "That is the most delicate and precise of all, and would require a year of toil on Breakness itself. At Pon it is impossible. Choose again."

"Evidently my life is to be one of many emergencies," said Beran. "The power of projecting energy from my hand might prove valuable."

"True," reflected Palafox. "And yet, on the other hand, what could more completely confuse your enemies than to see you rise into the air and float away? And since, with a novice, the easy projection of destruction endangers friends as well as enemies, we had better decide upon levitation as your first modification."

The surf-beaten cliffs of Nonamand rose from the ocean; they passed above a grimy fishing village, rode over the first ramparts of the Sgolaphs, flew low over the moors toward the central spine of the continent. Mount Droghead raised its cataclysmic crags; they swept close around the icy flanks, swerved down to the plateau of Pon. The car settled beside a long low building with rock-melt walls and a glass roof. Doors opened; Palafox floated the car within. They grounded on a floor of white tile; Palafox opened the port and motioned Beran out.

Beran hesitated, dubiously inspecting the four men who came forward. Each differed from the others in height, weight, skin- and hair-color, but each was like the others.

"My sons," said Palafox. "Everywhere on Pao you will find my sons. . . . But time is valuable, and we must set about your modification."

Beran alighted from the car; the sons of Palafox led him away.

They laid the anaesthetized body on a pallet, injected and impregnated the tissues with various toners and conditioners. Then standing far back, they flung a switch. There was a shrill whine, a flutter of violet light, a distortion of the space as if the scene were observed through moving panels of door glass.

The whine died; the figures stepped forward around the body now stiff, dead, rigid. The flesh was hard, but elastic; the fluids were congealed; the joints firm.

The men worked swiftly, with exceeding deftness. They used knives with entering edges only six molecules thick. The knives cut without pressure, splitting the tissues into glass-smooth laminae. The body was laid open halfway up the back, slit down either side through the buttocks, thighs, calves. With single strokes of another type of knife, curiously singing, the soles of the feet were removed. The flesh was rigid, like rubber; there was no trace of blood or body fluid, no quiver of muscular motion.

A section of lung was cut out, an ovoid energy-bank introduced. Conductors were laid into the flesh, connecting to flexible transformers in the buttocks, to processors in the calves. The antigravity mesh was laid into the bottom of the feet and connected to the processors in the calves by means of flexible tubes thrust up through the feet.

The circuit was complete. It was tested and checked; a switch was installed under the skin of the left thigh. And now began the tedious job of restoring the body.

The soles were dipped in special stimulating fluid, returned precisely into place, with accuracy sufficient to bring cell wall opposite cell wall, severed artery tight to severed artery, nerve fibril against nerve fibril. The slits along the body were pressed tightly together, the flesh drawn back into place over the energy bank.

Eighteen hours had passed. The four men now departed for rest, and the dead body lay alone in the darkness.

Next day the four men returned. The great machine whined again, and the violet light flickered around the room. The field which had gripped the atoms of Beran's body, in theory reducing his temperature to absolute zero, relaxed, and the molecules resumed their motion.

The body once more lived.

A week passed, while Beran, still comatose, healed. He returned to consciousness to find Palafox standing before the pallet.

"Rise," said Palafox. "Stand on your feet."

Beran lay quiet for a moment, aware by

some inner mechanism that considerable time had passed.

Palafox seemed impatient and driven by haste. His eyes glittered; he made an urgent gesture with his thin strong hand. "Rise! Stand!"

Beran slowly raised himself to his feet.

"Walk!"

Beran walked across the room. There was a tautness down his legs, and the energy-bulb weighed on the muscles of his diaphragm and rib-sheathing.

Palafox was keenly watching the motion of his feet. "Good," he exclaimed. "I see no halting or discoordination. Come with me."

He took Beran into a high room, hitched a harness over his shoulders, snapped a cord into a ring at his back.

"Feel here." He directed Beran's left hand to a spot on his thigh. "Tap."

Beran felt a vague solidity under his skin. He tapped. The floor ceased to press at his feet; his stomach jerked; his head felt like a balloon.

"This is charge one," said Palafox. "A repulsion of slightly less than one gravity, adjusted to cancel the centrifugal effect of planetary rotation."

He made the other end of the cord fast on a cleat. "Tap again."

Beran touched the plate, and instantly it

seemed as if the entire environment had turned end for end, as if Palafox stood above him, glued to the ceiling, as if he were falling head-first at the floor thirty feet below him. He gasped, flailed out his arms; the cord caught him, held him from falling. He turned a desperate glance toward Palafox, who stood faintly smiling.

"To increase the field, press the bottom of the plate," called Palafox. "To decrease, press the top. If you tap twice, the field goes dead."

Beran managed to return to the floor. The room righted, but swung and bobbed with nauseated effect.

"It will be days before you accustom yourself to the levitation mesh," said Palafox briskly. "Since time is short, I suggest that you practice the art diligently." He turned toward the door.

Beran watched him walk away, frowning in puzzlement. "Just why is time short, then?" he called to the spare retreating back.

Palafox swung around. "The date," he said, "is the fourth day of the third week of the eighth month. On Kanetsides Day I plan that you shall be Panarch of Pao."

"Why?" asked Beran.

"Why do you continually require that I expose myself to you?"

"I ask from both curiosity and in order to plan my own conduct. You intend that I be

Panarch. You wish to work with me." The gleam in Palafox's eyes brightened. "Perhaps I should say, you hope to work through me, in order to serve your ends. Therefore, I ask myself what these ends are."

Palafox considered him a moment, then replied in a cool even voice. "Your thoughts move with the deft precision of worm-tracks in the mud. Naturally I plan that you shall serve my ends. You plan, or, at any rate, you hope, that I shall serve yours. So far as you are concerned, this process is well toward fruition. I am working diligently to secure your birthright, and if I succeed, you shall be Panarch of Pao. When you demand the nature of my motives, you reveal the style of your thinking to be callow, captious, superficial, craven, uncertain and impudent."

Beran began to sputter a furious refutal, but Palafox cut him off with a gesture. "Naturally you accept my help—why should you not? It is only right to strive for your goals. But, after accepting my help, you must choose one of two courses: serve me or fight me. Forward my aims or attempt to deny me. These are positive courses. But to expect me to continue serving you from a policy of abnegation is negative and absurd."

"I cannot consider mass misery absurd," snapped Beran. "My aims are . . ."

Palafox held up his hand. "There is nothing

more to say. The scope of my plans you must deduce for yourself. Submit or oppose, whichever you wish. I am unconcerned, since you are powerless to deflect me."

Day after day Beran practiced the use of his modification, and gradually became adjusted to the sensation of falling head-first away from the ground.

He learned how to move through the air, by leaning in the direction he wished to travel; he learned how to descend, falling so fast the air sang past his ears, then braking with deft timing to land without a jar.

On the eleventh day, a boy in a smart gray cape, no more than eight years old, with the typical Palafox cast to his features, invited Beran to Palafox's apartments.

Crossing the concrete quadrangle, Beran armed his mind and arranged his emotions for the interview. He marched through the portal stiff with resolution.

Palafox was sitting at his desk, idly arranging polished trapezoids of rock crystal. His manner was almost affable as he directed Beran to a chair.

Beran warily seated himself.

"Tomorrow," said Palafox, "we enter the second phase of the program. The emotional environment is suitably sensitive: there is a general sense of expectation. Tomorrow, the quick stroke, the accomplishment! In a suitable manner we affirm the existence of the traditional Panarch. And then"—Palafox rose to his feet—"and then, who knows? Bustamonte may resign himself to the situation, or he may resist. We will be prepared for either contingency."

Beran was not thawed by unexpected cordiality. "I would understand better had we discussed these plans over a period of time."

Palafox chuckled genially. "Impossible, estimable Panarch. You must accept the fact that we here at Pon function as a General Staff. We have prepared dozens of programs of greater or less complexity, suitable for various situations. This is the first pattern of events to mesh with one of the plans."

"What, then, is the pattern of events?"

"Tomorrow three million persons attend the Pamalisthen Drones. You will appear, make yourself known. Television will convey your face and your words elsewhere on Pao."

Beran chewed his lips, angry both at his own uneasiness and at Palafox's indomitable affability. "What exactly is the program?"

"It is of the utmost simplicity. The Drones commence at an hour after dawn and continue until noon. At this time is the pause. There will be a rumor-passing, and you will be expected. You will appear wearing Black. You will speak." Palafox handed Beran a sheet of paper. "These few sentences should be sufficient."

Beran dubiously glanced down the lines of script. "I hope events work out as you plan. I want no bloodshed, no violence."

Palafox shrugged. "It is impossible to foretell the future. If things go well, no one will suffer except Bustamonte."

"And if things go poorly?"

Palafox laughed. "The ocean bottom is the rendezvous for those who plan poorly."

XV

ACROSS THE Hyaline Gulf from Eiljanre was Mathiole, a region of special and peculiar glamour. In the folktales of early Pao, when episodes of fantasy and romance occurred, Mathiole was inevitably the locale.

To the south of Mathiole was the Pamalisthen, a verdant plain of farms and orchards arranged like pleasure-glades. Here were seven cities, forming the apices of a great heptagon; and at the very center was Festival Feld, where drones took place. Among all the numerous gatherings, convocations and grand massings of Pao, the Pamalisthen Drones were accorded the highest prestige.

Long before dawn, on the Eighth Day of the Eighth Week of the Eighth Month, Festival Fields began to fill. Small fires flickered by the thousands; a susurration rose from the plain.

With dawn came throngs more: families gravely gay, in the Paonese fashion. The small children wore clean white smocks, the adolescents school uniforms with various blazons on the shoulders, the adults in the styles and colors befitting their place in society.

The sun rose, generating the blue, white and yellow of a Paonese day. The crowds pressed into the field: millions of individuals standing shoulder to shoulder, speaking only in hushed whispers, but for the most part silent, each person testing his identification with the crowd, adding his soul to the amalgam, withdrawing a sense of rapturous strength.

The first whispers of the drone began: long sighs of sound, intervals of silence between. The sighs grew louder and the silences shorter, and presently the drones were in full pitch—not-quite-inchoate progression, without melody or tonality: a harmony of three million parts, shifting and fluctuating, but always of definite emotional texture. The moods shifted in a spontaneous but ordained sequence, moods stately and abstract, in the same relationship to jubilation or woe that a valley full of mist bears to a fountain of diamonds.

Hours passed, the drones grew higher in pitch, rather more insistent and urgent. When the sun was two-thirds up the sky, a long black saloon-flyer appeared from the direction of Eiljanre. It sank quietly to a low eminence at the far end of the field. Those who had taken places here were thrust down into the plain, barely escaping the descending hull. A few curious loitered, peering in through the glistening ports. A squad of neutraloids in magenta and blue debarked and drove them off with silent efficiency.

Four servants brought forth first a black and brown carpet, then a polished black wooden chair with black cushioning.

Across the plain, the drones took on a subtly different character, perceptible only to a Paonese ear.

Bustamonte, emerging from the black saloon, was Paonese. He perceived and understood.

The drones continued. The mode changed once more as if Bustamonte's arrival were no more than a transient trifle—a slight more pungent, even, than the original chord of dislike and mockery.

Down the ordained progression of changes went the drones. Shortly before noon the sound ceased. The crowd quivered and moved; a sigh of satisfied achievement rose and died. The crowd changed color and texture, as all who could do so squatted to the ground.

Bustamonte grasped the arms of his chair to rise. The crowd was in its most receptive state, sensitized and aware. He clicked on his shoulder microphone, stepped forward to speak.

A great gasp came from the plain, a sound of vast astonishment and delight.

All eyes were fixed on the sky over Bustamonte's head, where a great rectangle of rippling black velvet had appeared, bearing the blazon of the Panasper Dynasty. Below, in mid-air, stood a solitary figure. He wore short black trousers, black boots, and a rakish black cape clipped over one shoulder. He spoke; the sound echoed over all Festival Field.

"Paonese: I am your Panarch. I am Beran, son to Aiello, scion of the ancient Panasper Dynasty. Many years I have lived in exile, growing to my maturity. Bustamonte has served as Ayudor. He has made mistakes—now I have come to supersede him. I hereby call on Bustamonte to acknowledge me, to make an orderly transfer of authority. Bustamonte, speak!"

Bustamonte had already spoken. A dozen neutraloids ran forward with rifles, knelt, aimed. Lances of white fire raced up to converge on the figure in black. The figure seemed to shatter, to explode; the crowd gasped in shock.

The fire-lances turned against the black rectangle, but this appeared impervious to the energy. Bustamonte swaggered truculently forward. "This is the fate meted to idiots, charlatans and all those who would violate the justice of the government. The imposter, as you have seen . . ."

Beran's voice came down from the sky. "You shattered only my image, Bustamonte. You must acknowledge me: I am Beran, Panarch of Pao."

"Beran does not exist!" roared. Bustamonte. "Beran died with Aiello!"

"I am Beran. I am alive. Here and now you and I will take truth-drug, and any who wishes may question us and bring forth the truth. Do you agree?"

Bustamonte hesitated. The crowd roared. Bustamonte turned, spoke terse orders to one of his ministers. He had neglected to turn off his microphone; the words were heard by three million people. "Call for police-craft. Seal this area. He must be killed."

The crowd-noise rose and fell, and rose again, at the implicit acknowledgement. Bustamonte tore off the microphone, barked further orders. The minister hesitated, seemed to demur. Bustamonte turned, marched to the black saloon. Behind came his retinue, crowding into the craft.

The crowd murmured, and then as if by a single thought, decided to leave Festival Field. In the center, at the most concentrated node, the sense of constriction was strongest. Faces twisted and turned; from a distance the effect was rapid pale twinkling.

A milling motion began. Families were wedged apart, pushed away from each other.

Then shouts and calls were the components of a growing hoarse sound. The fear became palpable; the pleasant field grew acrid with the scent.

Overhead the black rectangle disappeared, the sky was clear. The crowd felt exposed; the shoving became trampling; the trampling became panic.

Overhead appeared the police craft. They cruised back and forth like sharks; the panic became madness; screams became a continuous shrieking. But the crowd at the periphery was fleeing, swarming along the various roads and lanes, dispersing across the fields. The police craft swept back and forth indecisively; then turned and departed the scene.

Beran seemed to have shrunk, collapsed in on himself. He was pallid, bright-eyed with horror. "Why could we not have foreseen such an event? We are as guilty as Bustamonte!"

"It serves no purpose to become infected with emotion," said Palafox.

Beran made no response. He sat crouched, staring into space.

The countryside of South Minamand fell astern. They crossed the long narrow Serpent and the island Fraevarth with its bone-white villages, and swept out over the Great Sea of the South. Then the moors and the Sgolath crags, then around Mount Droghead to settle on the desolate plateau.

In Palafox's rooms they drank spiced tea, Palafox sitting in a tall-backed chair before a desk, Beran standing glumly by a window.

"You must steel yourself to unpleasant deeds," said Palafox. "There will be many more before the issues are resolved."

"What advantage to resolve issues, if half the people of Pao are dead?" asked Beran bitterly.

"All persons die. A thousand deaths represent, qualitatively, no more than one. Emotion increases merely in one dimension, that of intensity, but not of multiplicity. We must fix our minds on the final . . ." Palafox stopped short, tilted his head, listened to the speaker concealed inside his aural passages. He spoke in a tongue unknown to Beran; there was the inner reply, to which Palafox responded curtly. Then he sat back, regarding Beran with a kind of contemptuous amusement. "Bustamonte is settling your qualms for you. He has thrown a blockade around Pon. Mamarone was advancing across the plateau."

Beran asked in puzzlement. "How does he know that I am here?"

Palafox shrugged. "Bustamonte's spy service is efficient enough, but he vitiates it by his arrogant stupidity. His tactics are inexcusable. He attacks when clearly his best policy is compromise."

"Compromise? On what basis?"

"He might undertake a new contract with me, in return for the delivery of your person to the Grand Palace. He could thereby prolong his reign."

Beran was astounded. "And you would accede to this bargain?"

Palafox displayed wonder of his own. "Certainly. How could you think otherwise?"

"But your commitment to me—that means nothing?"

"A commitment is good only so long as it is advantageous."

"This is not always true," said Beran in a stronger voice than he had heretofore employed. "A person who fails one commitment is not often entrusted with a second."

"'Trust'? What is that? The interdependence of the hive; a mutual parasitism of the weak and incomplete."

"It is likewise a weakness," retorted Beran in fury, "to take advantage of trust in another—to accept loyalty, then fail to return it."

Palafox laughed in real amusement. "Be that as it may, the Paonese concepts of 'trust,' 'loyalty,' 'good faith' are not a part of my mental equipment. We dominie of Breakness Institute are individuals, each his own personal citadel. We expect no sentimental services derived from clan loyalty or group dependence; nor do we render any. You would do well to remember this."

Beran made no reply. Palafox looked at him curiously. Beran had stiffened, seemed lost in thought. In fact, a curious event had occurred inside his mind; there had been a sudden instant of dizziness, a whirl and a jerk which seemed to bypass an entire era of time, and he was a new Beran, like a snake sloughed of an old skin.

The new Beran turned slowly, inspected Palafox with dispassionate appraisal. Behind the semblance of agelessness, he saw a man of great age, with both the strengths and weaknesses of age.

"Very well," said Beran. "I necessarily must deal with you on this same basis."

"Naturally," said Palafox, but nonetheless with a trace of irritation. Then once more his eyes went vague; he tilted his head, listening to the inaudible message.

He rose to his feet, beckoned. "Come. Bustamonte attacks us."

They went out on a roof-top, under a transparent dome.

"There ..." Palafox pointed to the sky. "... Bustamonte's miserable gesture of ill-will."

A dozen of the Mamarone sky-sleds showed as black rectangles on the streaked gray sky. Two miles away a transport had settled and was exuding a magenta clot of neutraloid troops.

"It is well that this episode occurred," said Palafox. "It may dissuade Bustamonte from another like impertinence." He tilted his head, listening to the inner sound. "Now—observe our deterrent against molestation!"

Beran felt, or perhaps heard, a pulsating whine, so shrill as to be only partially in perception.

The sky-sleds began to act peculiarly, sinking, rising, jostling. They turned and fled precipitously. At the same time, there was excitement among the troops. They were in disarray, flourishing their arms, bobbing and hopping. The pulsating whine died; the Mamarone collapsed on the ground.

Palafox smiled faintly. "They are unlikely to annoy us further."

"Bustamonte might try to bomb us."

"If he is wise," said Palafox negligently, "he will attempt nothing so drastic. And he is wise at least to that extent."

"Then what will he do?"

"Oh—the usual futilities of a ruler who sees his regnum dwindling. . . ."

Bustamonte's measures in truth were stupid and harsh. The news of Beran's appearance flew around the eight continents, in spite of Bustamonte's efforts to discredit the occurrence. The Paonese, on the one hand drawn by their yearning for the traditional, on the other repelled by Bustamonte's sociological novelties, reacted in the customary style. Work slowed, halted. Cooperation with civil authority ceased.

Bustamonte attempted persuasion, grandiose promises and amnesties. The disinterest of the population was more insulting than a series of angry demonstrations. Transportation came to a standstill, power and communications died, Bustamonte's personal servants failed to report for work.

A Mamarone, impressed into domestic service, scalded Bustamonte's arms with a hot towel: this was the trigger which exploded Bustamonte's suppressed fury. "I have sung to them! They shall now sing in their turn!"

At random he picked half a hundred villages. Mamarone descended upon these communities and were allowed complete license.

Atrocity failed to move the population— already an established principle of Paonese history. Beran, learning of the events, felt all the anguish of the victims. He turned on Palafox, reviled him.

Palafox, unmoved, commented that all men die, that pain is transitory and in any event the result of faulty mental discipline. To demonstrate, he held his hand in a flame, the flesh burnt and crackled; Palafox watched without concern.

"These people lack this discipline—they feel pain!" cried Beran.

"It is indeed unfortunate," said Palafox. "I wish pain to no man, but until Bustamonte is deposed—or until he is dead—these episodes will continue."

"Why do you not restrain these monsters?" raged Beran. "You have the means."

"You can restrain Bustamonte as readily as I."

Beran replied with fury and scorn. "I understand you now. You want me to kill him. Perhaps you have planned this entire series of events. I will kill him gladly! Arm me, tell me his whereabouts—if I die, at least there shall be an end to all."

"Come," said Palafox; "you receive your second modification."

Bustamonte was shrunken and haggard. He paced the black carpet of the foyer, holding his arms stiff, fluttering his fingers as if to shake off bits of grit.

The glass door was closed, locked, sealed. Outside stood four black Mamarone.

Bustamonte shivered. Where would it end? He went to the window, looked out into the night. Eiljanre spread ghostly white to all sides. Three points on the horizon glowed angry maroon where three villages and those who had dwelt there felt the weight of his vengeance.

Bustamonte groaned, chewed his lip, fluttered his fingers spasmodically. He turned away from the window, resumed his pacing. At the window there was a faint hiss which Bustamonte failed to notice.

There was a thud, a draft of air.

Bustamonte turned, froze in his tracks. In the window stood a glaring-eyed young man, wearing black.

"Beran," croaked Bustamonte. *"Beran!"*

Beran jumped down to the black carpet, came quietly forward. Bustamonte tried to turn, tried to scuttle and dodge. But his time had come; he knew it, he could not move.

Beran raised his hand. From his finger darted blue energy.

The affair was accomplished. Beran stepped over the corpse, unsealed the glass doors, flung them aside.

The Mamarone looked around, sprang back, squinted in wonder.

"I am Beran Panasper, Panarch of Pao."

XVI

PAO CELEBRATED the accession of Beran in a frenzy of joy. Everywhere, except in the Valiant camps, along the shore of Zelambre Bay, at Pon, there was rejoicing of so orgiastic a nature as to seem non-Paonese. In spite of a vast disinclination, Beran took up residence in the Grand Palace and submitted to a certain degree of the pomp and ritual expected of him.

His first impulse was to undo all Bustamonte's acts, to banish the entire ministry to Vredeltope, the penal isle in the far north. Palafox, however, counseled restraint. "You act emotionally—there is no point in discarding the good with the bad."

"Show me something good," responded Beran. "I might then be less determined."

Palafox thought a moment, seemed to be on the point of speaking, hesitated, then said, "For instance: the Ministers of Government."

"All cronies of Bustamonte's. All nefarious, all corrupt."

Palafox nodded. "This may be true. But how do they comport themselves now?"

"Ha!" Beran laughed. "They work night and day, like wasps in autumn, convincing me of their probity."

"And so they perform efficiently. You would only work confusion in de-robing the lot. I advise you to move slowly—discharge the obvious sycophants and time-servers, bring new men into the ministry only whenever opportunity presents itself."

Beran was forced to admit the justice of Palafox's remarks. But now he sat back in his chair—the two were taking a lunch of figs and new wine on the palace roof garden—and seemed to brace himself. "These are only the incidental alterations I wish to make. My main work, my dedication, is to restore Pao to its former condition. I plan to disperse the Valiant camps to various parts of Pao, and do something similar with the Technicant installations. These persons must learn Paonese, they must take their places in our society."

"And the Cogitants?"

Beran rapped his knuckles on the table. "I want no second Breakness on Pao. There is scope for a thousand institutes of learning— but they must be established among the Paonese people. The must teach Paonese topics in the Paonese language."

"Ah yes," sighed Palafox. "Well, I expected nothing better. Presently I will return to Breakness, and you may restore Nonamand to the shepherds and furze-cutters."

Beran concealed his surprise at Palafox's docility. "Evidently," he said at last, "you plan something quite different. You assisted me to the Black Throne only because Busta-monte would not cooperate with you."

Palafox smiled to himself as he peeled a fig. "I plan nothing. I merely observe and, if requested to do so, advise. Whatever is to occur stems from plans long ago formulated and given momentum."

"It may become necessary to frustrate these plans," said Beran.

Palafox ate his fig without concern. "You are naturally at liberty to make such attempts."

During the next few days Beran pondered at great length. Palafox seemed to regard him as a predictable quantity, one which would automatically react in a direction favorable to Palafox. This consideration moved him to caution and he delayed immediate action against the three non-Paonese enclaves.

Bustamonte's splendid harem he sent packing, and began the formation of his own. It was expected of him; a Panarch without suitable concubines would be regarded with suspicion.

Beran felt no disinclination on this score; and since he was young, well-favored, and a popular hero, his problem was not so much one of seeking as of selection.

However, the affairs of state left him little time for personal indulgence. Bustamonte had overcrowded the penal colony on Vredeltope, with criminals and with political offenders mingled indiscriminately. Beran ordered an amnesty for all except confirmed felons. In the latter part of his reign, Bustamonte likewise had raised taxes until they approached those of Aiello's reign, with peculant officials absorbing the increment. Beran dealt decisively with these, setting the peculators to unpleasant types of menial labor, with earnings applied to their debts.

One day, without warning, a red, blue and brown corvette dropped down from space. The sector monitor issued the customary challenge; the corvette, disdaining response other than to break out a long serpent-tongue banderole, landed with insolent carelessness on the roof of the Grand Palace.

Eban Buzbek, Hetman of the Batmarsh Brumbos, and a retinue of warriors debarked. Ignoring the palace preceptors, they marched to the great throneroom, called loudly for Bustamonte.

Beran, arrayed in formal black, entered the hall.

By this time Eban Buzbek had heard a report of Bustamonte's death. He gave Beran a hard quizzical stare, then called to an interpreter. "Inquire if the new Panarch acknowledges me his overlord."

To the interpreter's timid question, Beran made no reply.

Eban Buzbek barked out, "What is the new Panarch's reply?"

The interpreter translated.

"In truth," said Beran, "I have no reply ready. I wish to reign in peace, still I feel that the tribute to Batmarsh has been paid long enough."

Eban Buzbek roared a quick gust of laughter when he heard the interpreter's translation. "This is not the manner in which realities arrange themselves. Life is a pyramid—only one may stand at the top. In this case it is I. Immediately below are others of the Brumbo Clan. In the remaining levels I have no interest. You must win the stage to which your prowess entitles you. My mission here is to demand more money from Pao. My expenses are increasing—therefore, the tribute must increase. If you agree, we part in amity. If not, my restive clansmen will visit Pao and you will regret your obstinacy."

Beran said, "I have no alternative. Under

protest I pay you your tribute. I will say also
that you would profit more as a friend to us
than as an overlord."

In the Batch tongue the word "friend" could
only be interpreted as "companion-in-arms."
Upon receiving Beran's reply, Eban Buzbek
laughed. "Paonese as companions-at-arms?
They who turned up their rumps for a kicking
when so ordered? Better warriors are the
Dinghals of Fire Planet, who march behind a
shield of their grandmothers. No—we Brumbos
have no need of such an alliance."

Retranslated into Paonese, the words became what seemed a series of gratuitous insults. Beran swallowed his wrath. "Your money
shall be transmitted to you." He bowed stiffly,
turned, strode from the room. One of the warriors, deeming his conduct disrespectful, leapt
forward to intercept him. Beran's hand came
up, his finger pointed—but again he restrained
himself. The warrior somehow sensed that his
doom had been close at hand, and stood back.

Beran left the hall unmolested.

Beran, trembling with anger, went to the
quarters of Palafox, who displayed no great
interest at the news. "You acted correctly,"
he said. "It is hopeless quixotry to defy such
experienced warriors."

Beran assented gloomily. "No question but
what Pao needs protection against brigands. . . .

Still, we are well able to afford the tribute, and it is cheaper than maintaining a large military establishment."

Palafox agreed. "The tribute is a decided economy."

Beran searched the long lean face for the irony he suspected, but finding none, took his leave.

The next day, after the Brumbos had departed, he called for a map of Shraimand, and studied the disposition of the Valiant camps. They occupied a strip along the coast ten miles wide by a hundred long, although the hinterland area had been depopulated another ten miles in anticipation of their increase.

Recalling his term of duty at Deirombona, Beran remembered the ardent young men and women, the tense faces, the steady undeviating expressions, the dedication to glory. . . . He sighed. Such traits had their uses.

He called Palafox to him, and began arguing heatedly, although Palafox had said nothing. "Theoretically, I agree to the need of an army, and also an efficient industrial establishment. But Bustamonte's procedure is cruel, artificial, disruptive!"

Palafox spoke gravely. "Suppose that by some miracle you were able to recruit, train and indoctrinate a Paonese army—then what? Whence will come their weapons? Who will supply warships? Who will build instruments and communications equipment?"

"Mercantil is the present source of our needs," Beran said slowly. "Perhaps one of the out-cluster worlds might supply us."

"The Mercantil will never conspire against the Brumbos," said Palafox. "And to procure merchandise from an out-cluster world, you must pay in suitable exchange. To acquire this foreign exchange, you must engage in trading."

Beran gazed bleakly from the window. "When we have no cargoships, we can not trade."

"Precisely true," said Palafox, in high good humor. "Come, I would show you something of which you are perhaps not aware."

In a swift black torpedo, Palafox and Beran flew to Zelambre Bay. In spite of Beran's questions, Palafox said nothing. He took Beran to the eastern shore, to an isolated area at the root of Maesthgelai Peninsula. Here was a group of new buildings, stark and ugly. Palafox landed the boat, took Beran inside the largest. They stood before a long cylinder.

Palafox said, "This is the secret project of a group of advanced students. As you have deduced, it is a small space-ship. The first, so I believe, ever built on Pao."

Beran surveyed the vessel without comment. Clearly Palafox was playing him as a fisherman plays a fish.

He went closer to the ship. The finish was rough, the detailing crude; the general impression, however, was one of rugged serviceability. "Will it fly?" he asked Palafox.

"Not now. But undoubtedly it shall—in another four or five months. Certain delicate components are on order from Breakness. Aside from these, it is a true Paonese production. With such a fleet of ships you may make Pao independent of Mercantil. I do not doubt that you will find sufficient trade, since the Mercantil screw the maximum advantage from any transaction."

"Naturally, I am—gratified," said Beran reluctantly. "But why was this work held secret from me?"

Palafox held up his hand and spoke in a soothing voice. "There was no attempt to keep you from knowledge. This is one project of many. These young men and women attack the problems and lacks of Pao with tremendous energy. Every day they undertake something new."

Beran grunted skeptically. "As soon as possible, these isolated groups shall be returned into the main current of Paonese life."

Palafox demurred. "In my opinion, the time is hardly ripe for any dilution of Technicant enthusiasm. Admittedly there was inconvenience to the displaced population, but the results seem to vindicate the conception."

Beran made no reply. Palafox signaled to the quietly observing group of Technicants. They came forward, were introduced, showed mild surprise when Beran spoke to them in their own language, and presently conducted him through the ship. The interior reinforced Beran's original conception of rough but sturdy serviceability. And when he returned to the Grand Palace it was with an entirely new set of doubts and speculations in his mind. Could it be possible that Bustamonte had been right, and he, Beran, wrong?

XVII

A YEAR WENT BY. The prototype space-ship of the Technicants was completed, tested and put into service as a training ship. On plea of the Technicant Coordinating Council, public funds were diverted to a large-scale ship-building program.

Valiant activity proceeded as before. A dozen times Bern decided to curtail the scope of the camps, but on each occasion the face of Eban Buzbek appeared to his mind's-eye and his resolve diminished.

The year saw great prosperity for Pao. Never had the people fared so well. The civil service was uncharacteristically self-effacing and honest; the taxes were light; there was none of the fear and suspicion prevalent during Bustamonte's reign. In consequence the population lived with almost non-Paonese gusto. The neolingual enclaves, like tumors, neither benign nor malignant, were not forgotten, but tolerated. Beran paid no visit to the Cogitant Institute at Pon; he knew however that it had expanded greatly; that new buildings were rising, new halls, dormitories, workshops, laboratories—that the enrollment increased daily, derived from youths arriving from Breakness, all bearing an unmistakable resemblance to Lord Palafox, and from other youths, rather younger, graduating from the Institute créches—children of Palafox and children of his children.

Another year passed, and down from space came the gay-colored corvette of Eban Buzbek. As before, it ignored the challenge of the monitor, and landed on the roof-deck of the Grand Palace. As before, Eban Buzbek and a swaggering retinue marched to the great hall, where they demanded the presence of Beran. There was a delay of ten minutes, during which the warriors stamped and jingled impatiently.

Beran entered the rooms, and halted, surveying the clansmen, who turned cold-eyed faces toward him.

Beran came forward. He made no pretense of cordiality. "Why do you come to Pao this time?"

As before, an interpreter transferred the words into Batch.

Eban Buzbek sat back into a chair, motioned Beran to another nearby. Beran took the seat without comment.

"We have heard unpleasant reports," said Eban Buzbek, stretching forth his legs. "Our allies and suppliers, the artifactors of Mercantil, tell us that you have lately sent into space a fleet of cargo-vessels—that you bargain and barter, and eventually bring back to Pao great quantities of technical equipment." The Batch warriors moved behind Beran; they towered over his seat.

He glanced over his shoulder, turned back to Eban Buzbek. "I cannot understand your concern. Why should we not trade where we will?"

"Sufficient should be the fact that it is contrary to the wish of Eban Buzbek, your liege-lord."

Beran spoke in a conciliatory voice. "But you must remember that we are a populous world. We have natural aspirations . . ."

Eban Buzbek leaned forward; his hand rang on Beran's cheek. Beran fell back into the chair, stunned by surprise, face white but for the red welt. It was the first blow he ever had received, his first contact with violence. The effect was peculiar—it was a shock, a stimulus, not altogether unpleasant, the sudden opening of a forgotten room. Eban Buzbek's voice sounded almost unheard: " . . . your aspirations must at all times be referred to Clan Brumbo for judgment."

One of the warriors of the retinue spoke.

"Only small persuasion is needed to convince the *ocholos*."

Beran's eyes once more focused on the broad red face of Eban Buzbek. He raised himself in his seat. "I am happy you are here, Eban Buzbek. It is better that we talk face to face. The time has come when Pao pays no further tribute to you."

Eban Buzbek's mouth opened, curved into a comical grimace of surprise.

"Furthermore, we shall continue to send our ships across the universe. I hope you will accept these facts in good spirit and return to your world with peace in your heart."

Eban Buzbek sprang to his feet. "I will return with your ears to hang in our Hall of Arms."

Beran rose, backed away from the warriors. They advanced with grinning deliberation. Eban Buzbek pulled a blade from his belt. "Bring the rascal here." Beran raised his hand in a signal. Doors slid back on three sides; three squads of Mamarone came forward, eyes like slits. They carried halberds with cusped blades a yard long, mounted with flame sickles.

"What is your will with these jackals?" the sergeant rasped.

Beran said, "Subaqueation. Take them to the ocean."

Eban Buzbek demanded the sense of the comments from the interpreter. On hearing it, he sputtered, "This is a reckless act. Pao shall be devastated! My kinsmen will leave no living soul in Eiljanre. We shall sow your fields with fire and bone!"

"Will you then go home in peace and bother us no more?" Beran demanded. "Come, the choice is yours. Death—or peace."

Eban Buzbek looked from right to left; his warriors pressed close together, eyeing their black adversaries.

Eban Buzbek sheathed his blade with a decisive snap. He muttered aside to his men. "We go," he said to Beran.

"Then you choose peace?"

Eban Buzbek's mustaches quivered in fury. "I choose—peace."

"Then throw down your weapons, leave Pao and never return."

Eban Buzbek, wooden-faced, divested himself of his arms. His warriors followed suit. The group departed, herded by the neutraloids. Presently the corvette rose from the palace, darted up and away.

Minutes passed; then Beran was called to the telescreen. Eban Buzbek's face glowed, glistening with hate. "I left in peace, young Panarch, and you shall have peace—only so long as it takes to bring the clansmen back to Pao. Not only your ears but your head will be mounted among our trophies."

Beran said, "Come at your own risk."

*   *   *

Three months later the Batch clansmen attacked Pao. A fleet of twenty-eight warships, including six round-bellied transports, appeared in the sky. The monitors made no attempt either to challenge or defend, and the Batch warships slid contemptuously down into the atmosphere.

Here they were attacked by rocket-missiles, but counter-missiles harmlessly exploded the barrage.

In tight formation, they settled toward north Minamand and landed a score of miles north of Eiljanre. The transports debarked a multitude of clansmen mounted on air-horses. They darted high into the air, dashing, cavorting, swerving in a fine display of braggadocio.

A school of anti-personnel missiles came streaking for them, but the defenses of the ships below were alert, and anti-missiles destroyed the salvo. However, the threat was sufficient to hold the riders close to the flotilla.

Evening came, and night. The riders wrote vain-glorious slogans in the sky with golden gas, then retired to their ships, and there was no further activity.

Another set of events had already occurred on Batmarsh. No sooner had the twenty-eight ship flotilla set forth for Pao, when another ship, cylindrical and sturdy, evidently converted from a cargo-carrier, dropped down into the dank forested hills at the south end of the Brumbo domain. A hundred young men disembarked. They wore ingenious segmented suits of transpar, which became streamlined shells when the wearer's arms hung by his sides. Anti-gravity mesh made them weightless, electric jets propelled them with great speed.

They flew low over the black trees, along the bottom of the wild valleys. Lake Chagaz glimmered ahead, reflecting the glowing constellations of the cluster. Across the lake was the stone and timber city Slagoe, with the Hall of Honors looming tall over the lesser buildings.

The flyers swooped like hawks to the ground. Four ran to the sacred fire, beat down the aged fire-tenders, quenched the blaze except for a single coal which they packed in a metal pouch. The remainder had continued past up the ten stone steps. They stunned the guardian vestals, charged into the tall smoky-beamed hall.

Down from the wall came the tapestry of the clan, woven with hair from the head of every Brumbo born to the clan. Helter-skelter into bags and gravity boxes went the trophies, the sacred fetishes: old armor, a hundred tattered banners, scrolls and declamations, fragments of rock, bone, steel and charcoal, vials of dried black blood commemorating battles and Brumbo valor.

When Slagoe at last awoke to what was taking place, the warriors were in space, bound for Pao. Women, youths, old men, ran to the sacred park, crying and shouting.

But the raiders had departed, taking with them the soul of the clan, all the most precious treasure.

On dawn of the second day the raiders brought forth crates and assembled eight battle-platforms, mounting generators, anti-missile defenses, dynamic stings, pyreumators and sonic ear-blasters.

Other Brumbo bravos came forth on air-horses, but now they rode in strict formation. The battle platforms raised from the ground and exploded. Mechanical moles, tunneling through the soil, had planted mines to the bottom of each raft.

The air-cavalry milled in consternation. Without protection they were easy targets for missiles—cowardly weapons by the standards of Batmarsh.

The Valiant Myrmidons likewise disliked missiles. Beran had insisted on every possible means to minimize bloodshed, but when the battle-rafts were destroyed, he found it impossible to restrain the Myrmidons. In their transpar shells they darted into the sky and plunged down at the Brumbo cavalry. A furious battle swirled and screamed over the pleasant countryside.

There was no decision to the battle. Myrmidons and Brumbo air-horsemen fell in equal numbers, but after twenty minutes, the air-horsemen suddenly disengaged and plunged to the ground, leaving the Myrmidons exposed to a barrage of missiles. The Myrmidons were not taken entirely unawares, and dove head-first for the ground. Only a few laggards—perhaps twenty—were caught and exploded.

The horsemen retreated under the shadow of their ships; the Myrmidons withdrew. They had been fewer than the Brumbos; nevertheless, the clansmen had given way, puzzled and awed by the ferocity of the resistance.

The remainder of the day was quiet, likewise the next day, while the Brumbos sounded and probed under the hulls of their ships to disengage any mines which might have been planted.

This accomplished, the fleet rose into the air, lumbered out over the Hylanthus Sea, crossed the isthmus just south of Eiljanre, settled on the beach within sight of the Grand Palace.

The next morning the Brumbos came forth on foot, six thousand men guarded by anti-missile defenders and four projectors. They moved cautiously forward, directly for the Grand Palace.

There was no show of resistance, no sign of the Myrmidons. The marble walls of the Grand Palace rose over them. There was motion on top; down rolled a rectangle of black, brown and tawny cloth. The Brumbos halted, staring.

An amplified voice came from the palace. "Eban Buzbek—come forth. Come inspect the loot we have taken from your Hall of Honors. Come forth, Eban Buzbek. No harm shall come to you."

Eban Buzbek came forth, called back through an amplifier. "What is this fakery, what cowardly Paonese trick have you contrived?"

"We possess all your clan treasures, Eban Buzbek: that tapestry, the last coal of your Eternal Fire, all your heraldry and relics. Do you wish to redeem them?"

Eban Buzbek stood swaying as if he would faint. He turned and walked unsteadily back to his ship.

An hour passed. Eban Buzbek and a group of noblemen came forth. "We request a truce, in order that we may inspect these articles you claim to have in your possession."

"Come forward, Eban Buzbek. Inspect to your heart's content."

Eban Buzbek and his retinue inspected the articles. They spoke no word—the Paonese who conducted them made no comment.

The Brumbos silently returned to their ships.

A nunciator called, "The time is at hand! Coward Paonese—prepare for death!"

The clansmen charged, driven by the most violent emotion. Halfway across the beach they were met by the Myrmidons, and engaged in hand to hand combat, with swords, pistols and bare hands.

The Brumbos were halted; for the first time their battle-lust met another more intense. They knew fear, they fell back, they retreated.

The voice from the Grand Palace called out, "You cannot win, Eban Buzbek, you cannot escape. We hold your lives, we hold your sacred treasures. Surrender now or we destroy both."

Eban Buzbek surrendered. He bent his head to the ground before Beran and the Myrmidon captain, he renounced all claim to Paonese overlordship, and kneeling before the sacred tapestry swore never more to molest or plan harm against Pao. He was then permitted the treasures of his clan, which the sullen clansmen carried aboard the flotilla, and departed Pao.

XVIII

TIME AFTER TIME Pao traced its orbit around Auriol, marking off five complex and dramatic years. For Pao at large they were good years. Never had living been so easy, hunger so rare. To the normal goods produced by the planet was added a vast variety of imports from far-off worlds. To every corner of the cluster the Technicant ships plied, and many a commercial battle was waged between Mercantili and Technicants. As a result, both enterprises expanded their services, and sought farther afield for trade.

The Valiants likewise became more numerous, but on a restricted basis. There was no further recruiting from the population at large, and only a child of Valiant father and mother could be received into the caste.

At Pon, the Cogitants increased in numbers, but even more slowly than the Valiants. Three new Institutes were established in the misty hills, and high upon the most remote crag of all Pao, Palafox built a somber castle.

The Interpreter Corps was now largely derived from the Cogitants; in fact, the Interpreters might be said to be the operative function of the Cogitants. Like the other groups, the Interpreters had expanded both in numbers and importance. In spite of the separation of the three neo-linguistic groups, from each other and from the Paonese population, there was a great deal of interchange. When an Interpreter was not at hand, the business might be transacted in Pastiche—which by virtue of its relative universality, was understood by a large number of persons. But when communication of any precision was necessary, an Interpreter was called for.

So the years passed, fulfilling all the changes conceived by Palafox, initiated by Bustamonte, and reluctantly supported by Beran. The fourteenth year of Beran's reign saw the high-tide of prosperity and well-being.

Beran had long disapproved of the Breakness concubinage system, which had taken unobtrusive but firm root at the various Cogitant Institutes.

Originally there had been no lack of girls to indenture themselves for eventual financial advantage, and all the sons and grandsons of

Palafox—not to speak of Palafox himself—
maintained large dormitories in the neighbor-
hood of Pon. But when prosperity came to
Pao, the number of young women available
for indenture declined, and presently peculiar
rumors began to circulate. There was talk of
drugs, hypnotism, black magic.

Beran ordered an investigation of the methods by which the Cogitants secured women
for indenture. He realized he would be tread-
ing on sensitive toes—but he did not suspect
the response would be so instant and so direct. Lord Palafox himself came to Eiljanre.

He appeared one morning on an upper terrace of the palace where Beran sat contemplating the sea. At the sight of the tall spare
frame, the angular features, Beran reflected
how little this Palafox differed, even to the
cloak of heavily brown cloth, the gray trousers, the peaked cap with a sharp bill, from
the Palafox he had first seen so many years
before. How old was Palafox?

Palafox wasted no time in preliminary small-
talk. "Panarch Beran, an unpleasant situation
has arisen, concerning which you will wish to
take steps."

Beran nodded slowly. "What is this 'unpleasant situation'?"

"My privacy has been invaded. A clumsy
gang of spies dogs my footsteps, annoys the
women in my dormitory with impertinent sur-

veillance. I beg that you discover who has ordered this persecution and punish the guilty party."

Beran rose to his feet. "Lord Palafox, as you must know, I personally ordered the investigation."

"Indeed? You astonish me, Panarch Beran! What could you hope to learn?"

"I expect to learn nothing. I hoped you would interpret the act as a warning, and make such changes in your conduct as the fact of the investigation would suggest. Instead you have chosen to contend the issue, which may make for difficulty."

"I am a Breakness Dominie. I act directly, not through devious hints." Palafox's voice was like iron, but the statement had not advanced his attack.

Beran, a student of polemics, sought to maintain his advantage. "You have been a valuable ally, Lord Palafox. In recompense, you have received what amounts to control over the continent of Nonamand. But this control is conditional upon the legality of your acts. The indenture of willing females, while socially offensive, is not a crime. However, when these females are unwilling . . ."

"What basis do you have for these remarks?"

"Popular rumor."

Palafox smiled thinly. "And if by chance you could verify these rumors, what then?"

Beran forced himself to stare into the obsidian gaze. "Your question has no application. It refers to a situation already of the past."

"Your meaning is obscure."

"The way to counter these rumors," said Beran, "is to bring the situation into the open. Henceforth, women willing to indenture themselves will appear at a public depot here in Eiljanre. All contracts will be negotiated at this depot, and any other traffic is declared a crime equivalent to kidnapping."

Palafox was silent several seconds. Then he asked softly, "How do you propose to enforce this decision?"

" 'Enforce'?" asked Beran in surprise. "On Pao it is not necessary to enforce the orders of the government."

Palafox curtly inclined his head. "The situation, as you say, is clarified. I trust neither of us will have cause for complaint." He took his departure.

Beran drew a deep breath, leaned back in his chair, closed his eyes. He had won a victory—to a certain degree. He had asserted the authority of the state and had wrung tacit acknowledgement of this authority from Palafox.

Beran was clever enough not to gloat. He knew that Palafox, utterly secure in his solipsism, probably felt nothing of the emotional umbra surrounding the occurrence, considered the defeat no more than a momentary irritation. Indeed, there were two highly significant points to consider: first, something in Palafox's manner which suggested that, in spite of his anger, he had been prepared to accept at least temporary compromise. "Temporary" was the key word. Palafox was a man biding his time.

Second, there was the phrasing of Palafox's last sentence: "I trust that neither of us shall have cause for complaint." Implicit was an assumption of equal status, equal authority, equal weight, indicating the presence of a disturbing ambition.

To the best of Beran's recollection Palafox had never so spoken before. Religiously he had maintained the pose of a Breakness dominie, temporarily on Pao as an advisor. Now it seemed as if he regarded himself a permanent inhabitant, with a proprietary attitude to boot.

Beran contemplated the events leading to the present tangle. For five thousand years Pao had been homogeneous, a planet directed by tradition, somnolent in an ageless tranquility. Panarchs succeeded each other, dynasties came and went, but the blue oceans and green fields were eternal. The Pao of these times had been easy prey for corsairs and raiders, and there had been much poverty.

The ideas of Lord Palafox, the ruthless dynamism of Bustamonte, in a single generation had changed all. Now Pao was prosperous and sent its merchant fleet cruising throughout the star-system. Paonese traders out-bargained the Mercantil, Paonese warriors out-fought the clansmen of Batmarsh, Paonese intellectuals compared favorably with the so-called wizards of Breakness.

But—these men who excelled, who out-traded, out-fought, out-produced, out-thought their planetary neighbors—were close to ten thousand and all had Palafox either for sire or grandsire. Palafoxians: A better name for these people!

The Valiants and the Technicants, what of them? Their blood was pure Paonese, but they lived as far from the stream of Paonese tradition as the Brumbos of Batmarsh or the Mercantil.

Beran jumped to his feet. How could he have been so blind, so negligent? These men were not Paonese, no matter how well they served Pao: they were aliens, and it was questionable where their ultimate loyalties lay.

The divergence between Valiant, Technicant and basic Paonese had gone too far. The trend must be reversed, the new groups assimilated.

Now that he had defined his ends, it was necessary to formulate the means. The problem was complex; he must move cautiously.

First of all—to establish the agency where women could present themselves for indenture. He would give Palafox no "cause for complaint."

XIX

AT THE EASTERN outskirts of Eiljanre, across the old Rovenone Canal, lay a wide commons, used principally for the flying of kites and festival mass-dancing. Here Beran ordered the erection of a large tent-pavilion, where women wishing to hire themselves to the Cogitants might exhibit themselves. Wide publicity had been given the new agency, and also to the edict that all private contracts between women and Cogitant would henceforth be illegal and felonious.

The opening day arrived. At noon Beran went to inspect the pavilion. On the benches sat a scattered handful of women, a miserable group by any standards, unlovely, harassed, peaked—perhaps thirty in all.

Beran stared in surprise. "Is this the lot of them?"

"That is all, Panarch!"

Beran rubbed his chin ruefully. He looked around to see the man he wished least to see: Palafox.

Beran spoke first, with some effort. "Choose, Lord Palafox. Thirty of Pao's most charming women await your whim."

Palafox replied in a light voice. "Slaughtered and buried, they might make acceptable fertilizer. Other than that, I see no possible use for them."

Implicit in the remark was a challenge: failure to recognize and answer it was to abandon the initiative. "It appears, Lord Palafox," said Beran, "that indenture to the Cogitants is as objectionable to the women of Pao as I had supposed. The very dearth of persons vindicates my decision." And Beran contemplated the lonely pavilion.

There was no sound from Palafox, but some intuition flashed a warning to Beran's mind. He turned his head, and his startled eyes saw Palafox, face like a death-mask, raising his hand. The forefinger pointed; Beran flung himself flat. A blue streak sizzled over head. He pointed his hand; his own finger-fire spat forward, ran up Palafox's arm, through the elbow, the humerus and out the shoulder.

Palafox jerked his head up, mouth clenched, eyes rolled back like a maddened horse. Blood sizzled and steamed where the mangled circuits in his arm had heated, fused and broken.

Beran pointed his finger once more; it was urgent and advisable to kill Palafox; more than this, it was his duty. Palafox stood watching, the look in his eyes no longer that of a human being; he stood waiting for death.

Beran hesitated, and in this instant, Palafox once more became a man. He flung up his left hand; now Beran acted and again the blue fire-pencil leapt forth; but it impinged on an essence which the left hand of Palafox had flung forth, and dissolved.

Beran drew back. The thirty women had flung themselves quaking and whimpering to the floor; Beran's attendants stood lax and limp. There was no word spoken. Palafox backed away, out the door of the pavilion; he turned and was gone.

Beran could find no energy to pursue. He returned to the palace, closed himself in his private rooms. Morning became the gold Paonese afternoon, day faded into evening.

Beran roused himself. He went to his wardrobe, dressed in a suit of skin-tight black. He armed himself with knife, hammer-beam, mind-blinder, swallowed a pellet of nerve-tonic, then unobtrusively made his way to the roof-deck.

He slipped into an air-car, wafted high into the night and flew south.

The dreary cliffs of Nonamand rose from the sea with phosphorescent surf at the base

and a few wan lights flickering along the top.
Beran adjusted his course over the dark up-
land moors toward Pon. Grim and tense he
sat, riding with the conviction that doom lay
before him.

There: Mount Droghead, and beyond, the
Institute! Every building, every terrace, walk,
out-building and dormitory was familiar to
Beran: the years he had served here as interpreter would now stand him in good stead.

He landed the car out on the moor, away
from the field, then activating the anti-gravity
mesh in his feet, he floated into the air and
leaning forward, drifted over the Institute.

He hovered high in the chill night wind, surveying the buildings below. There—Palafox's
dormitory, and there, through the triangular
translux panels, a glow of light.

Beran alighted on the pale rock-melt of the
dormitory room. The wind swept past, dron-
ing and whistling; there was no other sound.

Beran ran for the roof door. He burnt out the
seal with a flicker of finger-fire, slid the door
back, entered the hall.

The dormitory was silent; he could hear
neither voice nor movement. He set out down
the corridor with long swift steps.

The top floor was given over to the day
rooms, and was deserted. He descended a
ramp, turned to the right, toward the source
of the light he had seen from above. He stopped

outside a door, listened. No voices—but a faint sense of motion within: a stir, a shuffle.

He touched the latch. The door was sealed.

Beran readied himself. All must go swiftly. Now! Flick of fire, door free, door aside—stride forward! And there in the chair beside the table, a man.

The man looked up, Beran stopped short. It was not Palafox; it was Finisterle.

Finisterle looked at the pointed finger, then up to Beran's face. "What do you do here?" His exclamation was in Pastiche, and in this tongue Beran replied.

"Where is Palafox?"

Finisterle laughed weakly, let himself sink back into the chair. "It seems as if I nearly met the fate of my sire."

Beran came a step closer. "Where is Palafox?"

"You are too late. Palafox is gone to Breakness."

"Breakness!" Beran felt limp and tired.

"He is broken, his arm is a shred. No one here can repair him." Finisterle appraised Beran with cautious interest. "And this the unobtrusive Beran—a demon in black!"

Beran slowly seated himself. "Who could do it but I?" He glanced suddenly at Finisterle. "You are not deceiving me?"

Finisterle shook his head. "Why should I deceive you?"

"He is your sire!"

Finisterle shrugged. "This means nothing, either to sire or to son. A man, no matter how remarkable, has only a finite capability. It is no longer a secret that Lord Palafox has succumbed to the final sickness, he is an Emeritus. The world and his brain are no longer separate—to Palafox they are one and the same."

Beran rubbed his chin, frowned. Finisterle leaned forward. "Do you know his ambition, do you understand his presence on Pao?"

"I guess, but I do not know."

"Some weeks ago he gathered together his sons. He spoke to us, explained his ambition. He claims Pao as a world of his own. Through his sons, his grandsons, and his own capabilities, he will outbreed the Paonese, until eventually there will be only Palafox and the seed of Palafox on Pao."

Beran rose heavily to his feet.

"What will you do now?" asked Finisterle.

"I am Paonese," said Beran. "I have been passive in the Paonese fashion. But I have also studied at Breakness Institute, and now I shall act. And if I destroy what Palafox has worked so long to build—perhaps he will not return." He looked around the room. "I will start here, at Pon. You all may go where you will—but go you must. Tomorrow the Institute will be destroyed."

Finisterle leapt to his feet, restraint forgotten. "Tomorrow? This is fantastic! We can not leave our research, our library, our precious possessions!"

Beran went to the doorway. "There will be no more delay. You certainly have the right to remove your personal property. But the entity known as the Cogitant Institute will vanish tomorrow."

Esteban Carbone, Chief Marshal of the Valiants, a muscular young man with an open pleasant face, was accustomed to rise at dawn for a plunge into the surf.

On this morning he returned naked, wet and breathless from the beach, to find a silent man in black awaiting him.

Esteban Carbone halted in confusion. "Panarch, as you see, I am surprised. Pray excuse me while I clothe myself."

He ran to his quarters, and presently reappeared in a striking black and yellow uniform. "Now, Supremacy, I am ready to hear your commands."

"They are brief," said Beran. "Take a warship to Pon, and at twelve noon, destroy Cogitant Institute."

Esteban Carbone's amazement reached new heights. "Do I understand you correctly, Supremacy?"

"I will repeat: take a warship to Pon, destroy Cogitant Institute. Explode it to splinters. The Cogitants have received notice—they are now evacuating."

Esteban Carbone hesitated a perceptible instant before replying. "It is not my place to question matters of policy, but is this not a very drastic act? I feel impelled to counsel careful second thought."

Beran took no offense. "I appreciate your concern. This order, however, is the result of many more thoughts than two. Be so good as to obey without further delay."

Esteban Carbone touched his hand to his forehead, bowed low. "Nothing more need be said, Panarch Beran." He walked into his quarters, spoke into a communicator.

At noon precisely, the warship hurled an explosive missile at the target, a small cluster of white buildings on the plateau behind Mount Droghead. There was a dazzle of blue and white, and Cogitant Institute was gone.

When Palafox heard the news, his face suffused with dark blood; be swayed back and forth. "So does he destroy himself," he groaned between his teeth. "So should I be satisfied—but how bitter the insolence of this young coxcomb!"

The Cogitants came to Eiljanre, settling in the old Beauclare Quarter, south of the Rovenone. As the months passed they underwent a change, almost, it seemed, with an air of joyous relief. They relaxed the doctrinaire intensity which had distinguished them at the Institute, and fell into the ways of a bohemian intelligentsia. Through some obscure compulsion, they spoke little or no Cogitant, and likewise, disdaining Paonese, conducted all their affairs in Pastiche.

XX

BERAN PANASPER, Panarch of Pao, sat in the rotunda of the pink-colonnaded lodge on Pergolai, in the same black chair where his father Aiello had died.

The other places around the carved ivory table were vacant; no one was present but a pair of black-dyed neutraloids, looming outside the door.

There was motion at the door, the Mamarone's challenge in voices like ripping cloth. Beran identified the visitor, signaled the Mamarones to open.

Finisterle entered the room, gravely deigning no notice of the hulking black shapes. He stopped in the center of the room, inspected Beran from head to foot. He spoke in Pastiche, his words wry and pungent as the language itself. "You carry yourself like the last man in the universe."

Beran smiled wanly. "When today is over, for better or worse, I will sleep well."

"I envy no one!" mused Finisterle. "Least of all, you."

"And I, on the other hand, envy all but myself," replied Beran morosely. "I am truly the popular concept of a Panarch—the overman who carries power as a curse, delivers decisions as other men hurl iron javelins. . . . And yet I would not change—for I am sufficiently dominated by Breakness Institute to believe that no one but myself is capable of disinterested justice."

"This credence which you deprecate may be no more than fact."

A chime sounded in the distance, then another and another.

"Now approaches the issue," said Beran. "In the next hour Pao is ruined or Pao is saved." He went to the great black chair, seated himself. Finisterle silently chose a seat down near the end of the table.

The Mamarone flung back the fretwork door; into the room came a slow file—a group of ministers, secretaries, miscellaneous functionaries: two dozen in all. They inclined their heads in respect, and soberly took their places around the table.

Serving maidens entered, poured chilled sparkling wine.

The chimes sounded. Once more the Mamarone opened the door. Marching smartly into the room came Esteban Carbone, Grand Marshal of the Valiants, with four subalterns. They wore their most splendid uniforms and helms of white metal which they doffed as they entered. They halted in a line before Beran, bowed, stood impassively.

Beran had long realized this moment must come.

He rose to his feet, returned a ceremonious greeting. The Valiants seated themselves with rehearsed precision.

"Time advances, conditions change," said Beran in an even voice, speaking in Valiant. "Dynamic programs once valuable become harmful exaggerations when the need has passed. Such is the present situation on Pao. We are in danger of losing our unity.

"I refer in part to the Valiant camp. It was created to counter a specific threat. The threat has been rebuffed; we are at peace. The Valiants, while retaining their identity, must now be reintegrated into the general population.

"To this end, cantonments will be established among all the eight continents and the larger isles. To these cantonments the Valiants shall disperse, in units of fifty men and women. They shall use the cantonment as an organizational area and shall take up residence in the countryside, recruiting locally as becomes necessary. The areas now occupied by the Valiants will be restored to their previous use." He paused, stared from eye to eye.

Finisterle, observing, marveled that the man he had known as a moody hesitant youth should show such a strong face of decision.

"Are there any questions or comments?" asked Beran.

The Grand Marshal sat like a man of stone. At last he inclined his head. "Panarch, I hear your orders, but I find them incomprehensible. It is a basic fact that Pao requires a strong arm of offense and defense. We Valiants are that arm. We are indispensable. Your order will destroy us. We will be diluted and dispersed. We will lose our esprit, our unity, our competitivity."

"I realize all this," said Beran. "I regret it. But it is the lesser of the evils. The Valiants henceforth must serve as a cadre, and our military arm will once again be truly Paonese."

"Ah, Panarch," spoke the Grand Marshal abruptly, "this is the crux of the difficulty! You Paonese have no military interest, you . . ."

Beran held up his hand. "*We* Paonese," he said in a harsh voice. "All of us are Paonese."

The Grand Marshal bowed. "I spoke in haste. But, Panarch, surely it is clear that dispersion will lessen our efficiency! We must drill together, engage in exercises, ceremonies, competitions . . ."

Beran had anticipated the protest. "The

problems you mention are real, but merely pose logistical and organizational challenges. I have no wish to diminish either the efficiency or the prestige of the Valiants. But the integrity of the state is at stake, and these tumorlike enclaves, benign though they be, must be removed."

Esteban Carbone stared glumly at the ground a moment, then glanced left and right at his aides for support. The faces of both were bleak and dispirited.

"A factor you ignore, Panarch, is that of morale," Carbone said heavily. "Our effectiveness ..."

Beran interrupted briskly. "These are problems which you, as Grand Marshal, must solve. If you are incapable, I will appoint someone else. There will be no more discussion—the basic principle as I have outlined it must be accepted. You will confer with the Minister of Lands over details."

He rose to his feet, bowed in formal dismissal. The Valiants bowed, marched from the room.

As they left a second group entered, wearing the simple gray and white of the Technicants. They received, in general, the same orders as the Valiants, and put forward the same protests. "Why need the units be small? Surely there is scope on Pao for a number of industrial complexes. Remember that our efficiency depends on a concentration of skill. We cannot function in such small units!"

"Your responsibility is more than the production of goods. You must educate and train your fellow Paonese. There will undoubtedly be a period of confusion, but eventually the new policy will work to our common benefit."

The Technicants departed as bitterly dissatisfied as the Valiants.

Later in the day Beran walked along the beach with Finisterle, who could be trusted to speak without calculation as to what Beran might perfer to hear. The quiet surf rolled up the sand, retreated into the sea among glistening bits of shell, fragments of bright blue coral, strands of purple kelp.

Beran felt limp and drained after the emotional demands which had been made upon him. Finisterle walked with an air of detachment, and said nothing until Beran asked directly for his opinions.

Finisterle was dispassionately blunt. "I think that you made a mistake in issuing your orders here on Pergolai. The Valiants and Technicants will return to famlliar environments. The effect will be that of returning to reality, and in retrospect the instructions will seem fantastic. At Deirombona and at Cloeopter, the orders would have had more direct reference to their subject."

"You think I will be disobeyed?"

"The possibility appears strong."

Beran sighed. "I fear so myself. Disobedience may not be permitted. Now we must pay the price for Bustamonte's folly."

"And my sire, Lord Palafox's ambition," remarked Finisterle.

Beran said no more. They returned to the pavilion and Beran immediately summoned his Minister of Civil Order.

"Mobilize the Mamarone, the entire corps."

The Minister stood stupidly. "Mobilize the Mamarone? Where?"

"At Eiljanre. Immediately."

Beran, Finisterle and a small retinue flew down out of the cloudless Paonese sky to Deirombona. Behind them, still beyond the horizon, came six sky-barges, bearing the entire Mamarone corps, growling and mumbling to each other.

The air-car grounded. Beran and his party alighted, crossed the vacant plaza, passed under the Stele of Heroes, and entered the long low structure which Esteban Carbone used for his headquarters, as familiar to Beran as the Grand Palace at Eiljanre. Ignoring startled expressions and staccato questions, he walked to the staff room, slid back the door.

The Grand Marshal and four other officers looked up in an irritation which changed to guilty surprise.

Beran strode forward, impelled by an anger which overrode his natural diffidence. On the table lay a schedule entitled: *Field Exercises 262: Maneuver of Type C Warships and Auxiliary Torpedo-Units.*

Beran fixed Esteban Carbone with a lambent glare. "Is this the manner in which you carry out my orders?"

Carbone, after his initial surprise, was not to be intimidated.

"I plead guilty, Panarch, to delay. I was certain that after consideration you would understand the mistake of your first command . . ."

"It is no mistake. Now—at this very moment—I order you: implement the instructions I gave you yesterday!"

The men stared eye to eye, each determined to pursue the course he deemed vital, neither intending to yield.

"You press us hard," said the Marshal in a glacial voice. "Many here at Deirombona feel that we who wield the power should enjoy the fruits of power—so unless you wish to risk . . ."

"Act!" cried Beran. He raised his hand. "Or I kill you now!"

Behind him there was sudden movement, a spatter of blue light, a hoarse cry, a clatter of metal. Wheeling, Beran saw Finisterle standing over the body of a Valiant officer. A hammer-gun lay on the floor; Finisterle held a smoking energy-needle.

Carbone struck out with his fist, hit Beran hard on the jaw. Beran toppled back upon the desk. Finisterle turned to shoot, but was forced to hold his fire for the confusion.

A voice cried, "To Eiljanre! Death to the Paonese tyrants!"

Beran rose to his feet, but the Marshal had departed. Nursing his sore jaw, he spoke into a shoulder microphone; the six sky-barges, now above Deirombona, swooped down to the square; the monstrous black Mamarone poured forth.

"Surround the corps headquarters," came Beran's orders. "Allow neither entrance nor exit."

Carbone had broadcast orders of his own; from nearby barracks came hasty sounds, and into the plaza poured groups of Valiant warriors. At sight of the neutraloids they stopped short.

Squad leaders sprang forward; the Valiants became a disciplined force instead of a mob. For a space there was silence, while Mamarone and Myrmidon weighed each other.

At the necks of the squad leaders vibrators pulsed. The voice of Grand Marshal Esteban Carbone issued from a filament. "Attack and destroy. Spare no one, kill all."

The battle was the most ferocious in the history of Pao. It was fought without words,

without quarter. The Myrmidons outnumbered
the Mamarone, but each neutraloid possessed
three times the strength of an ordinary man.

Within the headquarters Beran called into
his microphone.

"Marshal, I beseech you, prevent this spill-
ing of blood. It is unnecessary, and good
Paonese will die!"

There was no response. In the plaza only a
hundred feet separated Mamarone from Myrmidon; they stood almost eye to eye, the
neutraloids grinning in humorless rancor, contemptuous of life, unconscious of fear; the Myrmidons seething with impatience and verve,
anxious for glory. The neutraloids, behind their
screens and with backs against the wall of the
corps headquarters, were secure from small
weapons; however, once they should move
away from the wall, their backs would be
vulnerable.

Suddenly they dropped the screens; their
weapons poured death into the nearby ranks:
a hundred men fell in an instant. The screens
returned into place and they took the retaliat-
ing fire without casualty.

The gaps in the front line were filled instantly. Horns blew a brilliant fanfare; the
Myrmidons drew scimitars and charged against
the black giants.

The neutraloids dropped the screens, the
weapons poured out death, a hundred, two

hundred warriors were killed. But twenty or thirty sprang across the final few yards. The neutraloids drew their own great blades, hacked, hewed; there was the flash of steel, hisses, hoarse calls, and again the Mamarone stood free. But while the shields had been down, lances of fire from the rear ranks of the Myrmidons found targets, and a dozen neutraloids were fallen.

Stolidly the black ranks closed. Again the Myrmidon horns sounded, again the charge, and again the hack and splinter of steel. It was late afternoon; ragged clouds low in the west veiled the sun, but an occasional beam of orange light played across the battle, glowing on the splendid fabrics, reflecting from glistening black bodies, shining dark on spilled blood.

Within the staff headquarters Beran stood in bitter frustration. The stupidity, the arrogance of these men! They were destroying the Pao he had hoped to build—and he, lord of fifteen billion, could find insufficient strength to subdue a few thousand rebels.

In the plaza the Myrmidons at last split the neutraloid line into two, battered back the ends, bunched the giant warriors into two clots.

The neutraloids knew their time had come, and all their terrible detestation for life, for men, for the universe boiled up and condensed

in a clot of pure fury. One by one they succumbed, to a thousand hacks and cuts. The
last few looked at each other, and laughed,
inhuman hoarse bellows, and presently they
too died, and the plaza was quiet except for
subdued sobbing. Then behind, by the Stele,
the Valiant women set up a chant of victory,
forlorn but exulting, the survivors of the battle,
gasping and sick, joined the paean.

Within the building Beran and his small com-
pany had already departed, flying back to
Eiljanre in the air-boat. Beran sat steeped in
misery. His body shook, his eyes burnt in their
sockets, his stomach felt as if it were caked
with lye. Failure, the breaking of his dreams,
the beginning of chaos!

He thought of Palafox's tall spare form, the
lean face with the wedge-shaped nose and
opaque black eyes. The image carried such
intensity of emotion to become almost dear to
him, something to be cherished from all harm,
except that destruction which he himself would
deal.

Beran laughed aloud. Could he enlist the
aid of Palafox?

With the last rays of sunset flickering over
the roofs of Eiljanre, he arrived at the Palace.

In the great hall sat Palafox, in his usual
gray and brown, a wry sad smile on his mouth,
a peculiar shine to his eyes.

Elsewhere in the hall sat Cogitants, Palafox's

sons for the most part. They were subdued, grave, respectful. As Beran came into the room, the Cogitants averted their eyes.

Beran ignored them. Slowly he approached Palafox, until they stood only ten feet apart.

Palafox's expression changed no whit; the sad smile trembled on his mouth; the dangerous shine glittered in his eyes.

It was clear to Beran that Palafox had completely succumbed to the Breakness syndrome. Palafox was an Emeritus.

XXI

PALAFOX SALUTED Beran with a gesture of apparent affability; but there was no corresponding change in his expression. "My wayward young disciple! I understand that you have undergone serious reverses."

Beran came forward another step or two. He need only raise his hand, point, expunge this crafty megalomaniac. As he marshaled himself to act, Palafox uttered a soft word, and Beran found himself seized by four men strange to him, wearing garments of Breakness. While the Cogitants looked on soberly these men flung Beran flat on his face, opened his clothes, touched metal to his skin. There was an instant of piercing pain, then numbness along his back. He heard the click of tools, felt the quiver of manipulation, a wrench or two, and then they were done with him.

Pale, shaken, humiliated, he regained his feet, rearranged his garmemts.

Palafox said easily, "You are careless with the weapon provided you. Now it is removed and we can talk with greater relaxation."

Beran could find no answer. Growling deep in his throat, he marched forward, stood before Palafox.

Palafox smiled slightly. "Once again, Pao is in trouble. Once again, it is Lord Palafox of Breakness to whom appeals are made."

"I made no appeals," said Beran in a husky voice.

Palafox ignored him. "Ayudor Bustamonte once needed me. I aided him, and Pao became a world of power and triumph. But he who profited—Panarch Beran Panasper—broke the contract. Now, again the Paonese government faces destruction. And only Palafox can save you."

Realizing that exhibitions of rage merely amused Palafox, Beran forced himself to speak in a voice of moderation. "Your price, I assume, is as before? Unlimited scope for your satyriasis?"

Palafox grinned openly. "You express it crudely but adequately. I prefer the world 'fecundity.' But such is my price."

A Cogitant came into the room, approached Palafox, spoke a word or two in Breakness. Palafox looked to Beran. "The Myrmidons are coming. They boast that they will burn Eil-janre, destroy Beran and set forth to conquer the universe. This, they claim, is their destiny."

"How will you deal with the Myrmidons?" asked Beran tartly.

"Easily," said Palafox. "I control them because they fear me. I am the most highly modified man on Breakness, the most powerful man ever to exist. If Esteban Carbone fails to obey me, I will kill him. To their plans for conquest I am indifferent. Let them destroy this city, let them destroy all the cities, as many as they will." His voice was rising—he was becoming excited. "So much the easier for me, for my seed! This is my world, this is where I shall live magnified by a million, a billion sons. I shall fructify a world; there never shall have been so vast a siring! In fifty years the planet will know no name other than Palafox, you shall see my face on every face. The world will be I, I will be the world!"

The black eyes glowed like opals, pulsing with fire. Beran became infected with the madness; the room was unreal, hot gases swirled through his mind. Palafox, losing the appearance of a man, took on various semblances in rapid succession: a tall eel, a phallus, a charred post with knotholes for eyes, a black nothingness.

"A demon!" gasped Beran. "The Evil Demon!" He lunged forward, caught Palafox's arm, hurled Palafox stumbling to the floor.

Palafox struck with a thud, a cry of pain.
He sprang to his feet holding his arm—the
same arm that Beran had wounded before—
and he looked an Evil Demon indeed.

"Now is your end, gad-fly!" He raised his
hand, pointed his finger. From the Cogitants
came a mutter.

The finger remained pointed. No fire leapt
forth. Palafox's face twisted in passion. He
felt his arm, inspected his finger. He looked
up, calm once more, signaled to his sons. "Kill
this man, here and now. No longer shall he
breathe the air of my planet."

There was dead silence. No one moved.
Palafox stared incredulously; Beran looked
numbly about him. Everywhere in the room
faces turned away, looking neither toward
Beran nor Palafox.

Beran suddenly found his voice. He cried
out hoarsely, "You talk madness!" He turned
to the Cogitants. Palafox had spoken in Breakness, Beran spoke in Pastiche.

"You Cogitants! Choose the world you would
live in! Shall it be the Pao you know now, or
the world this Emeritus proposes?"

The epithet stung Palafox; he jerked in anger, and in Breakness, the language of insulated intelligence, he barked, "Kill this man!"

In Pastiche, language of the Interpreters, a
tongue used by men dedicated to human service, Beran called, "No! Kill this senile megalomaniac instead!"

Esteban Carbone shrugged. "This is no great matter. We speak a few words of Pastiche, enough to make ourselves understood. Soon we will speak better, and so shall we train our children."

Beran spoke for the first time. "I offer a suggestion which perhaps will satisfy the ambitions of everyone. Let us agree that the Valiants are able to kill as many Paonese as they desire, all those who actively oppose them, and so may be said to exercise authority. However, they will find themselves embarrassed: first, by the traditional resistance of the Paonese to coercion, and secondly, by inability to communicate either with the Paonese or the Technicants."

Carbone listened with a grim face. "Time will cure these embarrassments. We are the conquerors, remember."

"Agreed," said Beran in a tired voice. "You are the conquerors. But you will rule best by disturbing the least. And until all Pao shares a single language, such as Pastiche, you cannot rule without great disturbance."

"Then all Pao must speak one language!" cried Carbone. "That is a simple enough remedy! What is language but a set of words? This is my first command: every man, woman and child on the planet must learn Pastiche!"

"And in the meantime?" inquired Finisterle.

Esteban Carbone chewed his lip. "Things

must proceed more or less as usual." He eyed
Beran. "Do you, then, acknowledge my power?"

Beran laughed. "Freely. In accordance with
your wish, I hereby order that every child of
Pao: Valiant, Technicant, Cogitant and Paonese,
must learn Pastiche, even in precedence to
the language of his father."

Esteban Carbone stared at him searchingly,
and said at last. "You have come off better
than you deserve, Beran. It is true that we
Valiants do not care to trouble with the details of governing, and this is your one bar-
gaining point, your single usefulness. So long
as you are obedient and useful, so long may
you sit in the Black Chair and call yourself
Panarch." He bowed, turned on his heel,
marched from the hall.

Beran sat slumped in the Black Chair. His
face was white and haggard, but his expression was calm.

"I have compromised, I have been humiliated," he said to Finisterle, "but in one day I
have achieved the totality of my ambitions.
Palafox is dead, and we are embarked on the
great task of my life—the unifying of Pao."

Finisterle handed Beran a cup of mulled
wine, drank deep from a cup of his own. "Those
strutting cockerels! At this moment they parade around their stele, beating their chests,
and at any instant . . ." He pointed his finger
at a bowl of fruit. Blue flame lanced forth; the
bowl shattered.

"It is better that we allowed them their triumph," said Beran. "Basically, they are decent people, if naïve, and they will cooperate much more readily as masters than as subjects. And in twenty years. . . ."

He rose to his feet; he and Finisterle walked across the hall, looking out over the roofs of Eiljanre. "Pastiche—composite of Breakness, Technicant, Valiant, Paonese. Pastiche—the language of service. In twenty years, everyone will speak Pastiche. It will fertilize the old minds, shape the new minds. What kind of world will Pao be then?"

They looked out into the night, across the lights of Eiljanre, and wondered.

THE BEST IN SCIENCE FICTION

THE TOR DOUBLES

Two complete short science fiction novels in one volume!